CHANGING LOCKS

EXTRA-ORDINARY MIDLIFE, BOOK 2

LYNN M. STOUT

CHAPTER 1

I awoke with cat hair stuck to my lips.

"Gross, Lex! What are you doing?"

The cat was standing on my chest, using my face to scratch his.

"Where's Gladys?" I picked another hair from the lip balm that worked a little too well.

Lex's large green eyes stayed focused on mine for a beat, then he shifted his gaze slightly to the left.

I didn't want to, yet I knew I had to look.

There, in the corner of the room, hovered the wispy form of what used to be the hostess of the bed-and-breakfast where I was staying.

"Oh, Gladys." I sat up and ran my hands through my hair.

She continued to float in the corner. I knew from experience that it would probably be awhile before she could control how she looked or even be able to speak. She was obviously distraught, wringing her see-through hands in front of her see-through body, opening and closing her mouth while no sounds came out.

"Hold on. I got you."

I pushed the cat off of me and threw back the covers.

I scanned the room, my eyes landing on the most horrific thing in my life at the moment, which was saying a lot. No matter how long it had been, it still rankled my nerves. It was the taxidermy beaver my deceased husband Joe had made almost twenty years ago.

"Joe? Can you help?"

His familiar form rose from the beaver, much like Jeannie from her bottle, and then took shape in front of me.

He shot me a dirty look, most likely still angry from the day before, but when he saw Gladys, his face registered confusion and then compassion. He went to her.

The ghostly conversation took only a few minutes, then Joe turned back to me.

"She said this happened way too soon and we need to help her get rid of Maybelle. Oh, and she wants you to take care of her cat," he said.

I shook my head. "Get rid of Maybelle? Why? How? And, no, I don't want a cat. I'm not set up for it. Surely someone else-,"

"She said to take care of the cat here and soon."

I sputtered.

"Here? What do you mean?"

"She wants you to take over the bed-and-breakfast and take care of the cat here."

"In Michigan?"

It seemed impossible, but two ghosts rolled their eyes at me at the same time.

"Duh," was Joe's eloquent response.

They shared a few more words, and then that was it. She disappeared and Joe, still scowling, told me the rest.

"She wanted you to help her get rid of Maybelle before she died, but she thinks there was foul play, and she was killed in her sleep before she could get your help. She's

2

anxious about being in the same house and is afraid of Maybelle. Also, she said someone would come in the next day and explain everything about the house and the cat."

He drifted back towards Brodie, but I stopped him.

"Joe, wait. Thank you for helping. And, I'm sorry. About everything."

He paused and seemed to think. Then he nodded and turned back.

"Thanks for that. There's something else though," he paused again. "There's something wrong here. I can't quite figure it out, but something is definitely off. There's more to all of this." He waved his hand in the air.

"Like what? Off how?"

He shrugged and faced Brodie.

"I don't think that was really Gladys."

CHAPTER 2

$\mathcal{I}$t was a little less than one week before the demise of the woman previously known as Gladys. We were zooming along I-96 from the airport on our way to a lovely little bed-and-breakfast I'd found on the outskirts of Detroit. The original plan was to stay in the city within walking distance of the conference we were there to attend, but this place kept popping up every time I looked. Finally, I gave in and booked it. It was a short drive and with the money we were saving, we could easily afford a taxi or car service each day.

Because of our work and our reputations, we were chosen to attend this conference created specifically for those who can see ghosts, as well as psychics, mediums, and even witches.

Charleston, our home, is a notoriously haunted old southern city that kept us all busy at work. Samantha was the expert in old homes, especially the antebellum style that made up a good part of Charleston. Tawny was the expert in encouraging unwanted spirits to leave, and I was on my way to being a mix of both of them and getting better at it every day.

I was gaining a reputation as the one who could remove your cranky ghost, or mediate between you and said ghost to bring peace. For the more adventurous souls, I was becoming rather adept at finding the perfect match between currently haunted houses and the buyers who love them.

Initially, Samantha was jealous of Tawny. She feared they had hired Tawny to replace her at the agency. When she discovered the truth that they actually hired Tawny to do the same job I was currently doing, the same job Samantha herself had gotten me, her jealousy shifted to being jealous of our relationship and what we had in common. It didn't help that Tawny was the picture of Samantha, just thirty years younger.

For the longest time, the only thing they had in common was the amount of makeup they wore and the height of their heels. After Joe passed, they both realized they had a lot more in common, namely me.

Joe, my husband of over thirty years, died unexpectedly from a heart attack while at work. The irony is that he was a heart surgeon. There wasn't much they could do, and it was over quickly. When I went to see him at the morgue in the hospital, his spirit attached to me and unbeknownst to me, I brought him home. There he connected to a taxidermy beaver he had made ages ago. He named the thing Brodie.

Brodie the Beaver stood about two feet tall and weighed roughly twenty pounds. He stood on a piece of wood that resembled a surf board. He wore a Hawaiian shirt, a gold chain around his neck, and a pair of sunglasses. Finally, he held his paws in a Shaka sign, thumb and pinky sticking out, other fingers folded down, reminiscent of the surfing culture of the sixties and seventies. Forever reminding us to "take it easy" and "hang loose." He became the conduit for my deceased husband's ghost to travel with me. And that's exactly what he did. He sat in the aisle seat during our recent flight from Charleston to Detroit, eliciting grins and chuckles from everyone who passed.

Now Samantha sat in the front seat of the car that picked us up at the airport, talking the ear off the poor driver. Tawny and I sat in the backseat, Brodie the Beaver propped up between us. The driver kept glancing in the rearview mirror as we drove along, understandably disturbed by the image.

The inertia shifted, and we took the exit more quickly than I would have preferred. As we leaned to the side, Tawny put a hand on Brodie, holding him steady. It was a sweet gesture. She and Joe were bonding. He liked her and said she reminded him of our kids, close in age and all. That's where the similarities stopped, however.

Their childhoods were very different.

Tawny grew up under the tutelage of her mother, Orenda, who taught her all she needed to know about her gifts and abilities. She was confident and intelligent and had no problem letting Sam or me know when she was taking charge.

My own children grew up as I did, under a strict moratorium that kept us from developing, or even acknowledging, our own abilities. The moratorium placed on my family was to not practice witchcraft, but even those of us who didn't really view ourselves as witches were stifled. My own mother kept me quiet and unobtrusive for my entire childhood.

Thankfully Tawny's mother, Orenda, was more than willing to help fill in the blanks.

She explained the moratorium and why it was placed on us. She told me about a terrible accident that occurred well over a hundred years ago. Someone in my family placed a curse on an evil, dangerous boy, ultimately trapping his spirit in his house for eternity. Sadly, his little sister was in the house at the time of the curse and she died as well. She was an innocent soul ultimately punished for her brother's crimes. It caused so many problems and heartache that when the council found out, their only recourse was to stop us from practicing until everything had time to settle.

That explained why no one told me when my young children began seeing ghosts. They told their grandmother, who promptly told them to ignore the ghost in their room. I'm sure she thought this was good advice, since the children's own abilities were obviously emerging and practicing for us was strictly forbidden. Still, I would have appreciated being looped in to their discoveries and finding out about our ancestry sooner. As a result, I worried I held the kids back from being all they could be because I didn't understand my own abilities. And even if I did, they were suppressed.

So here I was, fresh off a flight spent sitting in the middle seat between a perky, impudent, ghost hunting twenty-something named Tawny and the spirit of my deceased husband, Joe, currently residing in a taxidermy beaver. All while my best friend, Samantha, pretended not to know us and sat several rows ahead.

As we passed one empty building after another, my mood shifted. Weeds and shrubs did their best to overtake the crumbling brick facades. Most of the windows were broken or gone altogether. The buildings stood as empty hulking figures on the landscape. Once they were bustling with activity, with people moving in and out of them, teeming with energy as average men and women worked to provide comfortable lives for their families. Now, they were empty and haunted.

I saw the spirits of those who came before. Vague figures going about their daily grind, as though they didn't know what happened to them or to their city. A few seemed to know something was wrong, and I'd catch glimpses of them standing where a window once was, staring out, looking for something or someone. Or just maybe just looking for answers.

As Samantha continued to chat nonstop, and the driver continued to cast desperate glances in the rearview mirror, Tawny and I shared looks of concern and understanding. She was seeing the spirits and other beings, too.

We were used to the sounds and sights of Charleston, with its ghost stories of unsettled spirits, but no one talks as much about Detroit or Michigan in general. Or if they do, it didn't make it to my ears eight hundred miles to the south.

We finally pulled off the highway and entered a suburban area. Now, rather than large, empty buildings dotting the landscape, we saw huge, old homes on what were once luxurious streets. They were trying so hard. Street after street showed every third or fourth house being renovated, a concept dear to my heart. But the houses that weren't being renovated were consigned to the blight removal program and reluctantly awaited their turn.

As devastating as the abandoned buildings were, the houses were even more so. I ached for the families whose lives were turned upside down, and I couldn't imagine the moment when the parents looked at each other and knew they had to leave. Just leave it all behind. No jobs meant no money to pay the mortgage, no money for doctors, no money for groceries. They had to leave to survive. How had something like that happened in America?

We stopped at a stop sign, and Tawny and I both saw it at the same time. In the house on our right, in the attic, was a window missing glass. A figure swung from a rope around his neck, swaying slowly from side to side in front of the opening.

Tawny reached around Brodie the Beaver and held my hand.

~

The trip, which started out with laughter and excitement, turned to heartache and hopelessness. I swiped at an escaped tear and wondered how to help these lost souls. I knew Tawny was thinking the same thing. Samantha was oblivious to her surroundings until we pulled onto the street where our bed-and-breakfast was located.

"Adorable!"

Tawny and I both jumped at the sudden exclamation from the front seat.

Indeed, we seemed to have entered some type of portal to another dimension. Where the other one consisted of street after street, neighborhood after neighborhood of communities struggling to survive and revive, now we had entered technicolor. Large homes with wide porches lined the street. Fresh paint, bright flowers and deep green grass created a blindingly brilliant display. It was a mixture of styles and ages. It was obvious there used to be a lot of land around each home. Over time, the land was sold, and they built more homes closer to each other. There was a mixture of clapboard farmhouses and Gothic styles, with the occasional cottage and craftsman thrown in.

Our driver slowed in front of a very large, three-story Queen Anne home.

Samantha squealed.

"Is this it?" She asked. She turned around, throwing an arm over the front seat so she could see me. "Where did you find this place?"

I had to think for a moment. I didn't actually remember finding it. It's not as though I looked. Lisabeth asked me to book a hotel in Detroit as close to the conference as I could. I remember every single time I went into my computer to make the booking, or to even look at area hotels, this place was already up on the screen. I never actually looked for it, it just appeared. And in a very out of character move, I didn't overthink the decision. One day, the information was filled in and I simply hit the "Book" button and it was done.

"It just sort of popped up," I lamely explained.

"Well done!" Samantha said. "It's precious!"

Tawny looked at me with obvious curiosity, but her gaze shifted towards the house as the driver pulled up the long drive.

I stared up at the large wraparound porch and marveled at the elaborately decorated columns that appeared to have hand carved embellishments at the top of the arches. A turret set in the front left corner jutted over the steep roof. From the ground, it looked as though it might topple over any second.

"Wonder who gets that room," Samantha nodded her head towards the questionable architectural embellishment.

I could tell much of the original siding and wood shingles had been replaced with modern vinyl siding in a modest blueish grey color with a brick red fish scale design under the peak. Unpainted stone added another traditional layer of texture. Lace lattice work, almost black, adorned the giant three part window that showcased, for the entire neighborhood, what was going on inside the house.

"It looks like a giant gingerbread house," Tawny announced.

She wasn't wrong.

The owner, a sweet little old lady named Gladys Walker, met us on the front porch.

Short and stout, she smelled like chocolate chip cookies and looked like she ate them regularly. She was dressed all in pink from head to toe. She wore pink tennis shoes, and I caught a glimpse of pink socks. She wore pink pants and a pink polka-dot shirt with the sleeves pushed up to her elbows. A pair of shell pink glasses hung around her neck and she had a pink bandanna tied around her head.

She beamed as we piled out of the car.

"Oh, goodness! Welcome, welcome." Then she looked directly at me. "I've waited so long for you."

We'd only made the reservations a week ago, so I'm not sure how long she was waiting, but it didn't matter. It was a lovely reception and one that I was grateful for after our long flight.

Tawny and Samantha pulled suitcases and bags from the trunk, and I unbuckled Brodie from the backseat. Hiking him under my arm, I reached with my free hand to pull my suitcase along with me.

"I'm the only one who didn't want to bring this thing. Why am I the one who's stuck lugging it around?"

Neither of them heard me, or more likely they chose to ignore me, and they walked into the house. Gladys paused, one hand holding the door open and her right foot dancing back and forth as her cat attempted to dodge past her and through the open door.

"Get back, Lex," she chided. She looked at me a little impatiently, silently willing me to hurry and climb the stairs before her cat escaped.

I was going as fast as I could.

"Good grief, he's huge!" I exclaimed at the sight of the giant grey and white tuxedo cat.

"Naw," Gladys said. "He only looks big because he's fluffy. He only weighs seven pounds."

I shot a look at Samantha, who was hiding her laugh behind her hand. There was no way that cat weighed seven pounds. He was easily pushing twenty. And what Gladys thought was fluff was actually fat. Maybe some muscle underneath, but the slowly blinking green eyes that followed me around told me there wasn't much muscle. This was a huge, lazy, grey and white cat.

Tawny wasn't as enamored as I was. She kept looking sideways at Lex and was conspicuously keeping her distance from him. I would have to remember to ask her if she's allergic. I've always loved cats and was happy to have one here. Joe was allergic and so we never had one.

Gladys hustled us through the front parlor and up the stairs to our rooms. I was eager for a tour of the house, but even more eager to put Brodie down. I wrestled him around the two ninety-degree turns in the narrow staircase as our hostess explained we would have the entire house to ourselves for the week.

"I only have the four rooms to rent and you all took three of them. No one booked the fourth, which is fine with me. I sleep in an addition off the back of the house," she added.

Gladys paused outside one room and opened the door. I started to walk into it, desperate to put Brodie down, but she stopped me with an arm thrust across the opening.

"Nope. That's not your room."

I stepped back quickly, afraid I'd somehow offended her. She seemed to be nonplussed though and motioned for Tawny or Samantha.

"Either of you can have this one."

She turned and continued to walk down the hall. Sam and Tawny stared at each other and the room, then Tawny nudged Sam.

"You take it," she said.

Sam nodded and began dragging her modern luggage into the beautiful antique room. I tried to see more of the room, but Gladys called back impatiently.

"Come on. Let's get you two settled now. Let's go."

Tawny was dutifully following, and I took a few quick steps to catch up. By now I had worked up a decent sweat, and Brodie's wooden surfboard was frequently banging into the wall. I tried to keep him upright, but the weight and the weariness of the trip were weighing on me.

"Where is my room?" I asked tentatively.

Gladys ignored me and made a grand gesture, welcoming Tawny to her room. Again, I tried to see more detail of the exquisite area, but the door was closed decisively after Tawny entered.

It seemed that my room was special, and I was getting impatient to see it. Samantha and Tawny's spaces were gorgeous. Based on the brief glances I could steal, they had dark wooden floors covered with lush wine colored rugs. Luxurious bedding covered dark cherry sleigh beds. And I thought I saw a velvet covered chaise in both rooms, but it was hard to tell. I really hoped my room had everything I'd already glimpsed, and maybe even a little more, considering the work it was taking to get there.

"Is it this one?" I asked, hopefully pointing to the third door at the end of the hallway.

"One more flight," Gladys replied.

I tried not to cry.

"You have the most special room in the house," she spoke low, almost talking to herself. "Just you wait. You'll see."

I didn't answer, not quite certain it was me she was talking to.

Thinking through the layout of the house from what I could tell when outside, it appeared I was to be the "lucky" one who would spend the next week in the turret bedroom.

13

Samantha will have a great time making fun of me, but honestly, I was getting more and more excited. I loved old houses. I loved everything about this one so far, although I'd seen very little of it aside from the staircase. This place had stood for over a century and so far, so good. I pushed my fears aside and chose to embrace the experience. It was unlike any other I'd ever had and was exactly what I needed after the past year. Something unique, special and exquisite, just for me. Well, me and Brodie-Joe.

We finally stood outside the door, Gladys beaming with pride, me bouncing a little with excitement. With a great deal of fanfare, she flung the door open wide.

It looked as though someone had drawn a line down the middle of the room, then gave two monkeys pink and yellow paint and zero supervision.

The pink side had pink accents on the painted furniture, an old-fashioned chest of drawers, again painted white with pink trim. A lamp sat on the top, sporting a dark pink lampshade with white stripes and little pink balls hanging from the fringe. Even the rug had shades of pink ranging from very pale to almost rose. It was the bedroom of a little girl.

The other side was identical, except, of course, it was yellow.

There was no elaborately engraved cherry or walnut bed, either. Instead, a painted white queen sized bed sat against the flat part of the room, opposite the turret, which was also painted and decorated with the two colors. And I'm not sure how she managed to do it, but the coverlet over the bed was also split down the middle into the two colors. It looked like someone had sewn the two sides together.

I resisted the urge to shade my eyes and squint. The brightness of the colors and the obvious mismatched combination were a lot to take in. Especially after the long trip and the climb up the stairs. The headache that had been threatening all day finally popped into the forefront and I rubbed my temples.

Gladys turned to me. A look of excitement and happiness on her face.

"Don't you just love it?" She squealed.

"Yes," I stammered. "It's very interesting." And then, knowing I should have known better, I asked the question anyway. "Why the two colors?"

Gladys clapped her hands like a giddy child and literally bounced her ancient body across the room. She grasped a photo, an eight by ten in a pink and yellow frame, and brought it close for me to see.

In it were two little girls, twins from the look of it, although the photo was in black and white. They were dressed identically and had their hair in pigtails. They posed the same, and they had the same smile.

"Who is this?" I asked.

"Well, that's me," Gladys said, peering over my shoulder and pointing a pink-colored fingernail at the photo. "And that is my twin sister, Maybelle."

"Oh, I didn't know you had a sister! How lovely!"

"She died," Gladys said abruptly. "A long time ago. I don't have a sister anymore. But this was our room when we were very young. Before everything. I keep it mostly the way it was back then. A new bed, of course. We had twin beds."

With that last line, Gladys turned on her heel and strode from the bedroom, leaving me alone with Brodie the Beaver, an inordinate amount of pink and yellow making me dizzy and a growing headache poking the back of my eyeballs.

CHAPTER 3

*G*ladys slowly made her way back down the stairs. It had been years since she'd made the trek up both flights in one day. Thankfully, the cleaning service was available to get that top room ready. She never could have managed.

She needed to get moving though and have a snack and tea ready for her guests. She suspected the pretty one would come bounding down the stairs any second now, full of the energy of the young and stupid.

The other old one, Samantha, would be down soon too. Looking for her liquor, no doubt. She tried to remember if she'd already hidden the good stuff. A quick look at the liquor cart confirmed she had.

Connie, now that was another issue altogether. Gladys was fairly certain she would take a nap first, and she probably wouldn't emerge until much later.

"Move it, Lex," she pushed the cat out of the way. He was always underfoot when she was in the kitchen. The kitchen was the one room she had paid to fully modernize. It retained the old charm of a traditional Queen Anne kitchen. A long wooden table ran down the center of the room, serving as additional counter space. The counter tops themselves were made of granite and supported all the best appliances. It was a satisfying mix of old and new, and it made her happy. She hummed as she moved throughout the open room, preparing a snack and tidying up as she went.

She stood in front of the open pantry and stared into it for several seconds.

"What was I looking for?"

She wrinkled her nose to the side as she thought. Age was creeping up on her more and more each day. Thankfully, Connie was finally here and she could relax.

Soon she would get the help she needed and then it would all be over. She just had to keep it together for a little longer and then everything would click into place.

And speaking of clicking. She moved a few feet to her right and tried the other door that stood just next to the pantry. The handle was locked. She dug around in the junk drawer and found the key to the bolt. She inserted it and turned it hard to the left.

It was locked, too.

Good.

CHAPTER 4

"*J*oe? Come on out."

I started unpacking and organizing my things, then I went into the bathroom. My short, ever greying hair was a mess from the travel and from me running my hands through it with the impending headache. I smoothed the two streaks of grey that sprouted from the part in front and smiled at my reflection. I liked how my grey was coming in. Sam insisted I should have it colored. If I did, it would be to emphasize the grey, which would leave her mortified.

When I turned back, Joe was sitting on the bed. I still haven't figured out why he needs to sit. It's not like he has any weight to hold. He can float, for Pete's sake.

"Great room," he said with a smirk.

"Yeah, well, no thanks to you. Nice trick getting on the airplane, by the way."

"Hey, that wasn't my idea. Your friend showed up and grabbed me. And tell Samantha to be a little more careful. She almost broke off another finger."

He gestured towards the beaver that was sitting at the foot of the bed. The pinky finger on his right hand was twisted a little. I reached over and gently bent it back the way it was supposed to be.

"Can you feel that? I mean, it doesn't hurt, right?"

Joe laughed. "No, I can't feel it. But a guy wants to look nice when traveling with his wife, you know?"

I paused for a moment, surprised. It was strange having him refer to me as his wife. Our current relationship status was unique, and it all came about so quickly. Within a week of Joe's death, the moratorium was lifted and my abilities grew by leaps and bounds. Soon I could see and talk to him as though nothing had changed, and it was as though he never died. Instead, there was a slight blip on the radar. Then everything snapped back into place.

"Hey," he drifted closer to me. "Hey, I'm sorry. The wife thing. I guess that's still strange for you."

Once again, I wondered if he could read my mind. I nodded and smiled.

"Thanks," I said. "You're right. It's strange. But it's okay. We'll figure it out."

For the past year, I'd steadfastly avoided mourning my husband. After all, he was still with me. What was there to mourn? At least that's what I told myself. Added to that, I found I wanted him around, if only to help manage unruly ghosts.

"I'm going downstairs," I said. "You want to come?"

Joe shook his head. "No, I just make Samantha a nervous wreck, and Tawny won't stop staring at me. Or at Brodie. It's like she thinks he's going to animate suddenly." He paused and a sneaky smile spread across his face. "I'm going to try to do that. Freak them out."

We both laughed.

"Good luck. I can't wait to see it. If you can do it, that is."

It would be nice to see Tawny knocked off her high horse for once. She knew so much more than I did and I enjoyed her discomfort a little more than I should have. Samantha's too. She was the one who kept pushing the ghost theory to me after Joe died and was the first to actually state that she thought he was haunting me. Then, when it turned out to be true, she backpedaled faster than I've ever seen her move before.

I started for the door and stopped when Joe said, "Connie, be careful. It feels weird here."

"Yeah, I feel it too. I'll be careful."

I made my way downstairs and was greeted by a warm sight. Samantha and Tawny sat on velvet covered tufted chairs. Their legs stretched out with their heads resting on the high backs. They each held a drink. Tawny's was what looked like tea in a dainty teacup and saucer that she held with both hands. Samantha swirled her almost empty highball glass and looked skeptically at the inch of liquid left in the bottom.

They cheered when they saw me.

"What did I do?" I asked as I made my way to the sofa to sit across from them.

The seating was arranged so each seat faced the magnificent fireplace that provided warmth in the winter and otherwise served as the centerpiece of the room. The mantle was adorned with carvings and embellishments, and had the obligatory mirror sitting above.

"Gladys said you were sleeping."

"Yeah, we figured we wouldn't see you again until tomorrow morning. Way to rally," Tawny said, lifting her teacup in a mock toast.

"Well, I do have a headache knocking around, but I'll be okay. Not quite ready for bed at," I checked my watch, "four o'clock in the afternoon." I rolled my eyes and made a spectacle of throwing the back of my hand against my forehead in a fake faint.

"So, are we going out, then?" Tawny asked. She looked expectantly between me and Samantha.

Despite my exaggerated reaction to the implication that I was old, I was actually over twice her age and really my back, knees and that damn headache would not allow for it.

"You go if you want to." Samantha said. "I'm in for the night. This night, at least, maybe tomorrow."

"I agree. I'm not going anywhere," I added.

"Not by myself!" Tawny exclaimed. "How is that any fun?"

"No, that's a bad idea. She doesn't know the city and a pretty girl shouldn't be out at night by herself. How would it look? A guest from my house out on the town alone!"

Gladys appeared under the arched doorway that led to the dining area. She'd been listening to our conversation and obviously had a firm opinion of what she considered appropriate behavior for today's young woman.

Tawny opened her mouth to retort. I knew her well enough to know what was coming. She was undoubtedly going to say something about not caring how it "looked" and then possibly going into a rant about being an adult, and being able to take care of herself, etc.

Not wanting to alienate our host in the first hour of our arrival, I cut her off before she could begin.

"I think we will enjoy relaxing here tonight." I looked at Tawny. "We'll hit the town tomorrow night, okay? All three of us," I added with a nod towards Gladys.

Tawny grudgingly obliged, and Gladys seemed a little more excited than was fitting. She clapped her hands and did a little hop.

"Not long now and we'll eat," she announced over her

shoulder as she spun around and headed back towards what I assumed was the kitchen.

I could already smell food cooking, and my stomach grumbled.

"Where'd you get that drink?"

Samantha smiled and pushed herself up from her chair. Standing in front of the liquor cart, she put her finger over her lips and bent down. With a gentle tap of her finger, a small hidden door in the bottom of the cart swung open. Several bottles of high end bourbon, vodka and gin sparkled.

"So what's on top?" I asked.

"The cheap stuff." She grunted as she reached into the back of the cabinet and pulled out an elaborately decorated bottle of gin.

She expertly mixed two gin and tonics. Not my first choice, but when she placed the cold drink in my hand, I knew she'd made an excellent decision.

She hid everything back where she'd found it and settled back in her chair just seconds before Gladys reappeared.

"Dinner is ready," she announced.

The dining room was set with beautiful place settings. I'm not an expert in china but based on the ornate design on each plate and the obvious fragility of them, I knew they were unique and old. It was strange to be eating something as simple as pasta with meatballs off of the obvious antiques. But with a warm loaf of bread and a bottle of red wine, I got over it.

"We have more," Gladys trilled from the kitchen. "I'll bring more wine too!"

"I haven't even finished my gin and tonic," I mumbled to Samantha.

"Me either. It is a little early for dinner," she stated.

Tawny opened her mouth again, no doubt to comment on the early bird special she was sure we would enjoy. Samantha threw up a pointer finger and cocked her head with one eyebrow raised in a warning sign. Tawny took the hint and closed her mouth.

Gladys reappeared with another bottle of wine and more bread, then she took her seat at the head of the table. Samantha and I alternated between our gin and tonics and the wine as we ate. I knew I was going to pay for this later.

Gladys told us stories of the neighborhood as we ate. She didn't spare a bit of the gossip.

"My neighbor over there," she motioned to her right, "is a cabaret dancer. So you know what that means." She let her words hang in the air, apparently waiting for us to agree that we knew what that meant. Except we didn't.

"Too much makeup, red lipstick, short skirts, high heels. You know...," she continued. Then she made an exaggerated wink and sat back in her chair. Satisfied that the wink explained it all.

We nodded as though we understood.

She said the family on her left had recently moved in and seemed nice enough. Then she lowered her voice to barely a whisper and said, "They're Black."

Uncertain why she felt the need to whisper, or even why she felt the need to specify that information, I felt myself getting a bit hot. This always happened every time someone made an ignorant comment like that. I understood she was old and from another time, but by the same token, that comment gave off the prejudiced vibe and it drove me nuts. Ignoring Samantha's sharp look, I launched into my prepared speech, saved for occasions just like this. I informed Gladys that my future son-in-law is African American and I couldn't be more proud of him or my daughter.

As I spoke, she literally clutched her pink pearls.

23

Without another word, she stood and fumbled her way into the kitchen, muttering something about getting more wine for the table.

Samantha looked at me and shook her head.

"She's old, Connie. Let her be."

Tawny was shaking her head vehemently. "No, she did the right thing. You can't just let something like that go. No matter how old someone is. She needs to get with the times. And what was she implying about her neighbor? Does she think she's a sex worker? And why can't I go out by myself?"

I agreed with Tawny, but since her comments pulled Samantha's ire away from me, I said nothing. The two of them launched into a philosophical debate about systemic racism and what their roles as white women should be in fighting it. Then they moved onto gender equality and the role of each generation. They agreed in principle, but not in application. The age difference created quite the contrast.

I listened as they debated, vaguely interested, but I'd heard it all before. Get a few drinks in those two and they set out to right every wrong imaginable.

As they argued their points, I leaned back in my chair and stretched. A movement outside caught my eye. A man was standing on the sidewalk just in front of the house. From the dining room, I could barely see him all the way through the front windows. Normally, I don't think I would have noticed anything that far away, but he was being pretty obvious, moving back and forth and bobbing up and down as though dodging an attack. I didn't think he could see me since I was fairly deep in the house. Although with the large window, I supposed it was possible. I watched for a few more seconds, then he froze and stood stock still. He furtively peered up and down the street, turned, and walked out of my sightline.

Before I could tell Samantha and Tawny about the strange behavior, a composed Gladys reentered the room.

"Congratulations on the pending marriage of your daughter," she said formally.

I decided to be gracious and took it as her way of apologizing.

"Thank you."

Then I motioned with my thumb across the street and changed the subject. "I saw a man outside. It seemed like he was watching the house."

Gladys's nose curled up, and her lips pressed into a thin line. Her eyes narrowed as she looked past me towards the house.

"That's Thomas," she spat. "He lives across the street."

"He was acting strange," I said. "Like he was trying to sneak around or something."

"What's his deal?" Tawny asked from behind her hand. She stifled a yawn and rolled her eyes at Samantha's knowing look.

"He doesn't have a deal," Gladys said. "He's just a horrible, terrible, mean man. He hates me and I hate him."

"Wow, what did he do?" Samantha asked.

"What happened?" I echoed.

Gladys screwed up her face. "He killed my sister."

I'd always been able to feel when something was about to happen. I couldn't put a name to whatever it was, but I could tell if it would be good or bad and often, who it would affect. For years, my family teased me about my paranoia. Joe would tell me I was imagining things and when something happened that I predicted, he dismissed it as coincidence. I learned early and repeatedly that I had an overactive imagination and worried needlessly.

It wasn't until lately that I redefined what I felt. Now I called it intuition. Orenda and Tawny explained that it was a gift that I should practice and even improve. A gift that I should embrace, not suppress. And a gift I should certainly not be ashamed of or try to hide.

So, now, here I sat with my spidey sense tingling.

We weren't able to get any more information from Gladys after she announced Thomas killed her sister. Before we could form our questions, she turned and, oddly enough, skipped from the room with Lex on her heels. We heard a door slam and what sounded like a lock being turned, and then nothing else.

Samantha suggested we talk about it later, in private, since Gladys had already snuck up on us a few times. We agreed. Then, uncertain what the protocol was, we began clearing the table. Apparently, doing the dishes was left up to the guests. We made quick work of it, laughing and talking about the conference and our plans for the week.

Now we sat in Tawny's room. She lay on her bed, propped up by pillows. Samantha perched on a dressing chair. And I lounged in the velvet covered chaise I had glimpsed earlier that day.

"Well, that it was certainly unexpected," Tawny said, referring to Gladys's comment.

"There's more to the story, that's for sure," Samantha agreed.

I nodded as they spoke. They were both correct on all counts.

"Tawny, are you feeling anything?" I asked.

"Sure. We've had a fair amount to drink. I'm definitely feeling it."

"No, that's not what I mean. I mean 'feeling' anything?" I emphasized the word and added air quotes.

"Ah! Gotcha' and no, not really. Why?"

"Joe and I both are getting some weird sensations. Something seems to be off. I can't really explain it any more than that. My intuition is screaming at me. You're not feeling anything?"

Tawny shook her head slowly. "No, not really. Although I haven't tapped into anything intentionally. Sometimes if it's not overwhelming, I don't feel it until I concentrate. I'll focus tonight and see if I can pick up on what you're sensing."

"Thanks. Let me know."

"You know, if Thomas really murdered her sister, that might be what you're sensing," Samantha said.

"That's not a bad thought." She had a good point and a unique perspective.

"Oh, and before we go to bed, I need to climb those stairs and see the room you're in," she added.

"No, you really don't want to do that," I laughed. "Especially right before bed. You'll likely have nightmares."

"In the morning then," Samantha said.

"Good night."

"'Night."

"Sleep well."

Their two doors clicked quietly closed, and I stood at the foot of the stairs. Then I took a deep breath and began the steep climb to the pink and yellow hell that was my room.

I wasn't at all prepared for what I saw when I opened my door.

There, in the middle of the bedroom, stood Joe with another woman.

Jealousy stabbed my heart, quickly followed by anger and indignation.

Joe turned to me quickly. "It's not what you think."

"How do you know what I think?" I retorted. The words coming out before I could stop them.

Joe paused, caught off guard, then he laughed. Within a few seconds, my own shock wore off, and I understood what he found amusing.

The two ghosts weren't doing anything. They simply existed in the same space, in their nebulous forms, floating around the room.

The woman had no expression at all. Her eyes were wide and vacant. Her hair was in waves down her back. She looked young. Around the age of our oldest daughter, Hannah. Twenty-four or so.

My anger, hurt, and jealousy vanished. "Who is this?" I asked. I moved closer to them and the woman floated back away from me.

"I don't know," Joe said. "She appeared not too long ago and I've been trying to talk to her. She doesn't seem able to communicate. I don't know what else to try. You?"

I'd learned many ways to communicate with spirits and ran through a few options we could try. I brought an EVP with me. Of course, I had the ghost app that started this whole mess and was the very first way Joe communicated. It was still on my phone. Joe shook his head at each suggestion.

"Too technical. I'm getting the impression she's very naïve. And scared."

"Maybe Tawny can help," I offered as my last suggestion. Despite my experience with Joe, Tawny was still far and away the expert when it came to interacting with spirits, especially confused ones.

The woman looked from one to the other of us as we spoke. She looked as though she desperately wanted to speak, to add to the conversation and tell us something. And she looked familiar.

Then I realized. "Oh, how stupid of me! I'll bet it's Maybelle. Gladys's sister! Gladys told us tonight that Thomas, this guy across the street, killed her."

"What? What happened?"

"She didn't tell us anything else. She just said that and left the room. So if that's the case, if this is Maybelle and Thomas killed her, maybe he did it in this room. Or he moved her body here or something. I don't know how that works. But look, here's her picture."

I showed Joe what Gladys had shown me earlier that day. He agreed she looked like the same person, but it was hard to tell for sure. While they were twins, the picture we had was of them around eight years old. And we could compare to Gladys, who was eighty. But this spirit looked to be in her twenties and, of course, she was a spirit, so her features weren't the clearest.

She watched as she spoke, looking from one of us to the other.

"Can you answer questions?" I asked her.

She looked at me, eyes wide and staring.

"Are you Maybelle?" I asked.

"Can you talk to me?" Joe volunteered.

Without a word or any type of sign, she vanished.

"Where'd she go?" I asked Joe.

"How would I know?" Joe said with a tinge of attitude.

I ignored it and added, "So, I'm guessing she's not Maybelle?"

He shrugged.

Part of me wanted to ask him what was wrong. Something had shifted in the last few minutes. But the other part of me just wanted to go to sleep and not worry about the hurt feelings of my ghostly husband.

"I'm going to bed. I'm beat. And we've got a big day tomorrow."

"Yup," he said perfunctorily.

"Okay, then. Good night," I said and went into the bathroom to change.

When I came out, Joe was gone and Brodie the Beaver was still standing there, suggesting I take it easy.

I really hated that thing.

I crawled under the covers, pulling them up to my chin. I slept under the pink side of the covers.

The next morning was bright and chilly. It felt invigorating outside. Charleston was our home, and we had grown used to the humid wall of air that struck as soon as you opened a door. We all had forgotten how nice it was to not immediately begin sweating upon standing up first thing in the morning.

As we drank our coffee on the front porch, I saw Thomas open his front door and peek out.

I nudged Samantha and motioned with my head towards him. She kicked Tawny and got her attention, then did the same.

"Is that Thomas?" Tawny whispered.

"I think so. It definitely looks like the guy from last night."

The three of us watched him from our hiding place behind the shrubs that surrounded the porch.

He peered up and down the street. Then he disappeared

back into the house, only to reappear seconds later with a trash bag in his hands. It was a basic kitchen trash bag with red handle ties. He had it tied closed and was carrying it with both hands. He set off down the street.

It looked like he had a bowling ball, or a pumpkin, something that size and shape, in the bag.

We all looked at each other, then back at the man. He hurried along until he was about three houses away. He stopped in front of the trash can, furtively glanced around again, then hefted the bag up and into the neighbor's trash can.

"Is it a head?" Tawny asked in a whisper.

"Probably," Samantha said.

"Yeah, probably," I added.

"Oh, it most definitely is a head. I told you he's a terrible man. Wouldn't surprise me a bit if it's my sister's head in that bag."

Gladys's voice boomed through the morning air, causing us all to jump and spill coffee. Thomas heard her and held up his middle finger.

Gladys offered her own finger in greeting, yelled a few obscenities at the top of her lungs, then stormed back into the house, as the sound of profanities echoed throughout the quiet neighborhood.

I'm sure we looked as shocked as we felt. The three of us, sitting on the porch in a tidy row with our mouths hanging open. Before going into this own home, Thomas turned back to us. He raised his pointer finger and shook it. Then he slammed his door.

"At least we didn't get the same finger Gladys got," Samantha mumbled.

"Happens every morning." Yet another neighbor startled us.

"Crap!" Tawny jumped and spilled even more coffee. "What is up with this place?"

"I'm Reba. I live next door." The woman jabbed her thumb over her shoulder towards the house on the right.

"The cabaret dancer?" Tawny asked, her eyes twinkling with mischief even as she wiped coffee off her shirt.

I couldn't blame her. After Gladys's description the previous night, what we saw before us was not what we expected. Maybe at one time she had been a dancer, but now she was easily eighty years old. She wore a housedress and fuzzy slippers with a bandana wrapped around her hair curlers. There was no bright red lipstick, and I was certain her little feet hadn't seen high heels in ages. She leaned heavily on her walker, which was sinking into the grass.

"Back in the day," she replied to Tawny. "But not anymore. Now I wake up every day to a string of profanity from Gladys there. And she thinks I'm the harlot."

"Harlot! That's the word I was trying to think of last night," Tawny exclaimed.

"Really?" Samantha said, trying to encourage Reba to keep talking. "Profanity from Gladys? Why?"

"It's always been like this for as long as I can remember. I heard the story after I moved in. She's dead now though," her voice drifted lower.

"Who's dead?" Samantha asked, still trying to get answers.

"Maybelle."

"Maybelle was Gladys's sister, right?"

Reba nodded and moved towards us, leaning heavily on the railing. She abandoned her walker and began climbing the steps to the porch. Tawny hopped up and offered her an arm that was brusquely smacked away.

Reba huffed and puffed her way up the steps, then

plopped herself into the chair Tawny had just vacated. She continued her story as though nothing had happened.

"After Maybelle disappeared, Gladys went insane and blamed Thomas."

"Disappeared? I thought you said she died." Tawny said.

"Ah, but they never found a body," Reba said. "So officially they say she disappeared. And since there's no body, there's no way to charge Thomas. It's all gossip and hearsay. But do you want to know what I think happened?"

Samantha and I blurted out at the same time. "Yes!"

"Gladys and Thomas were quite an item back in the day. It was a great love story. Then they had a terrible fight and broke it off. Turns out Maybelle was driving a wedge between them. She was jealous. Thomas got angry at Maybelle for trying to break them up and he killed her. Gladys was so distraught that she couldn't bear to be with Thomas, and that was the end of that. Still, they live here, across the street from each other. That can't be easy. Although it's been this way for decades. Maybe they get a sort of comfort from it."

Reba finished her theory and pushed herself standing. "Either way, strange things happen here and ever since Maybelle's death, Gladys hasn't been the same. There's an edge to her. She's always angry. Although I guess that isn't so surprising. I might be angry too if my fiancé killed my sister. Have a good day."

She waved over her shoulder as she shuffled down the steps and lunged for her walker. Prying it from the grass with each step, she worked her way back across the lawn to her home.

"Well, now you know," Gladys said as she came back onto the porch.

"Were you listening the whole time?" I asked. We really had to be careful. Who knew what else she overheard?

33

She nodded. "It's easier to let someone else tell you. It's still so hard to talk about." She wiped at a tear that left a light pink trail through her heavily powdered cheek.

"How can you stand living across from him?" Samantha asked. "Can't you do something? Make him move?"

Gladys shook her head. "There's nothing I can do. He's threatened me too, you know. I'm a bit afraid of him. I know I act all brave but, well, he's capable of so much. Even at his age, I still don't trust him. In fact, if anything ever happens to me-," Her words drifted away, and she gazed at me.

I looked back, wondering what she was thinking and why she was looking at me so intently.

CHAPTER 5

*T*he twins stared at each other across the table.

"I can't believe you did that."

"So what? If he really loved you, it wouldn't have mattered."

"It matters because you're my sister. You're supposed to love me."

"You don't need me to love you, you have Thomas. Or are you afraid you'll lose him, too?"

"I wouldn't be afraid I'd lose him if my sister wasn't trying to come between us."

"You need to have more confidence in your relationship. You're being paranoid."

"No thanks to you. Stay away from him."

"Or what?"

"Or I'll make sure you stay away from him."

"I'd like to see you try."

CHAPTER 6

I tossed and turned all night long. The bed was uncomfortable, my neck was killing me, and the headache was still knocking around. Desperate, I even tried sleeping under the yellow side of the coverlet. That didn't help either. I had to get up, find an ibuprofen or four, and get some water. Before my feet hit the floor, I saw something that made me think I was still asleep and dreaming.

It was two little girls standing side by side. It reminded me of the twins in blue dresses, holding hands at the end of the hallway in The Shining. Except in this case, one wore a pink dress and one wore yellow.

And they were not holding hands.

Instead, the little girl in yellow was picking on the one in pink. I could only assume it was Maybelle picking on Gladys based on their signature colors. Maybelle pulled her hair and then pinched her. The little Gladys cried and tried to run away, but Maybelle cruelly grabbed her arm and twisted it.

How was it they were identical, but Maybelle seemed to be so much stronger than Gladys? And Gladys did nothing to fight back. I continued to watch them make their way around the room. Gladys constantly trying to get away and Maybelle chasing her down and torturing her.

After several minutes, I decided to intervene, if I even could. My mothering instincts were kicking in and I wanted to tell them to stop playing around.

"Where are you supposed to be?" I asked them. "Why are you running around up here?"

They both stopped and stared at me. Then they hung their heads and disappeared.

It was an hour before my alarm was set to go off, so I got up. I wasn't sleeping anyway and after that, there was no way I'd get back to sleep. After a quick shower, I wandered downstairs looking for coffee. Even if Gladys wasn't up yet, I planned to make some for myself and maybe even enjoy it with Lex beside me.

I needn't have worried. Gladys was indeed awake. Dressed today in a pink tracksuit with her pink tennis shoes, she flitted around the kitchen like a ball of pink bubblegum. Sticky and sweet.

"Good morning, sunshine!" She sang out.

"Good morning."

"Coffee?"

"Yes, please."

"You look tired, dear. Maybe you should go back to bed. It is very early."

I nodded. That had crossed my mind a few times as I showered. But now my hair was wet, and I didn't want to take the effort to dry it. Instead, I took my coffee and wandered into the sitting room.

"I'll just be in here if that's okay?"

Gladys nodded and bustled around me. "Here honey, have a little blanket. This will keep the chill away. Lex!"

I jumped when she yelled for the cat.

"Lex! Come keep Connie warm. Get to know her a little."

She smiled at me and bounced from the room. Not long after, Lex came ambling into the room. He stood just in front of me, his tail twitching back and forth. He stared at me as though I were doing something very wrong.

"Come on up, kitty." I made a scratching sound with my fingernails and clicked my tongue. He still stood. His look shifting from a stare to a glare.

"What?" I asked him. "What's wrong?"

Could you be more insulting?

I looked around the room for the voice. No one was there. I looked back at Lex, who was now sitting in front of me, his head to one side, eyes narrowed.

"Lex?" I asked quietly. "Did I just hear you?"

I waited a few seconds, and nothing happened. Maybe I imagined it. I was still tired and not completely awake yet. In fact, a part of me wouldn't have been surprised at all if I were still asleep, and all of this was just a continuation of last night's dream.

I set my coffee cup down and reached over. Lex was huge. Gladys was seriously in denial that he was simply fluffy. I grunted as I lifted the giant cat onto my lap.

He settled in quickly, turning a few circles, his claws digging into my thighs as he slipped around. Then he curled into a tight ball and purred. Loud and inconsistent. He sounded like an old coal train trying to make it up an especially steep hill. I think he stopped breathing at one point.

Keeping one hand on him to monitor signs of life, I reached for my coffee with the other. It was one of the most enjoyable mornings I'd had in a while. It was nice to be alone for a bit. Of course, I loved my friends and my family, but with Joe always around, traveling with Sam and Tawny and a busy work schedule, I missed having a little downtime.

I enjoyed Lex's erratic purring, and the warmth of his

body curled up on mine. The coffee was amazing and the morning crisp and cool, yet I was warm and content. Very little in the world is better than snuggling under a blanket with a cat. I would have to think about getting one when I returned home. A kitten, though. Something smaller.

I still wanted to get more details from Gladys after what she'd said the night before. Plus, the dream I'd had was fresh on my mind. I was certain the two were related, and there was more to this story. I just couldn't quite put my finger on it.

∿

Not long after that thought passed through my head, Tawny came bounding down the stairs. The energy in this child was off the charts. She said she was going for a run and scooted out of the front door before I could say anything.

Instead, I wondered how I was going to get up from the couch and out from under the cat. My back muscles weren't working and my feet were losing circulation. As the house was waking up, I was seriously considering going back to sleep.

I didn't think about it for long before Samantha came to my rescue.

"Good morning," she said.

I raised my coffee cup in greeting.

"You look very happy there. Good morning Lex." She scratched his head, just behind his ears. He lifted his face so she could scratch the white part under his chin. His purring got louder and Samantha sat beside me so she could get a better angle.

I smiled as I watched Lex wallow under her long fingernails.

"Sleep well?"

"No, not really," I said. "I was restless and achy. I think all the walking we did yesterday, especially after all the travel, has my neck messed up. And my back too. Plus, I had a strange dream where I thought I was awake. Then I actually woke up, and I was all...," I waved my hands around my head, then sighed.

"Oh, I hate that. I've done that before. It's so disconcerting. I'm sorry you had a rough night. Do you want to talk about the dream? Would that help?"

I nodded and shifted under the weight of Lex, which was apparently the wrong thing to do. He stood, shooting me an evil look that only a cat can master. Then he went to great lengths to rub himself against Samantha before he jumped down from the couch.

We laughed as Sam held my hand and hefted me up. Slowly, I shuffled behind her into the kitchen. I was looking for more coffee while Sam wanted her first cup.

Gladys was still preparing breakfast. It was very cozy and smelled wonderful. We decided to keep her company.

When we were settled at the kitchen table, Samantha said, "Tell me about your dream."

She added a dollop of cream to her coffee and swirled it carefully.

"Gladys, you might be interested in this." I caught her eye. "You were in it. Actually, you and your sister."

She dropped the plate she was carrying.

"Oh, dear. Oh, oh!"

Samantha was up in a flash, helping her clean up the mess. It wasn't as bad as it sounded, just a few crumbs and the plate didn't break, thankfully.

"I'm so sorry, Gladys," I exclaimed. "I didn't mean to upset you. Here, sit down."

Gladys sat, shivering.

"I should have been more sensitive," I said. "I wasn't

thinking. Of course, hearing that would upset you. I'm so sorry."

Gladys nodded along as I apologized and continued to stumble over my words, trying to find the right ones to express my sorrow. It became apparent Gladys was more angry than upset. After a minute, she interrupted.

"Well, what was the dream? Tell me what happened." She asked abruptly.

"Well, I think it was just the two of you," I began slowly for fear of angering her further. "It looked like Maybelle was maybe picking on you. Pulling your hair and pinching you. Kid stuff," I added, although it had looked more like bullying than simply sisters fighting.

"Did she do that?" Samantha asked.

"It looked kind of bad," I added carefully.

"Yes. It was. Awful. Excuse me." She pushed herself away from the table and turned her back towards us as she rummaged in a drawer. She must have found a key because next she was unlocking a nondescript door that was slightly recessed into the kitchen wall.

"Don't follow me."

She disappeared through the door and closed it with a solid thud. We heard her steps as she descended. Then a muffled voice rose through the floorboards. It was difficult to understand what she was saying, but it seemed she was still angry. Her voice rising and falling.

"Did I strike a nerve?" I asked Sam as we listened, eyes wide, ears straining to hear anything of use.

"I would say so," Tawny appeared in the doorway. "What did you say to her?" She pulled out a chair and sat down, breathing a little heavy.

I explained about my dream and telling Gladys about it.

"I guess it brought up terrible memories?"

I looked from one to the other as we all shrugged.

Tawny shook her head slowly, her eyes downcast, her body still. She was trying to listen to what Gladys was saying. She was still raging below us.

"I think-," Samantha started and was cut off by Tawny holding up one finger. Her bright purple polish flashed in the morning light as her other pointer finger went to her lips.

"Shhhh," she whispered.

I rolled my eyes at Sam, who was turning red in the face. While we'd learned to appreciate Tawny, it rankled both of us how she regularly and without inhibition shushed us. She also had no problem telling us what to do and pointing out when we did something wrong.

Honestly, it was our issue. Having my own children who were her age and knowing they would never speak to me like that was hard to reconcile. But, as Joe kindly pointed out one night when I was fuming about her precociousness, Tawny wasn't my child. She's my co-worker. My colleague. And she had valuable information and experience despite being half my age. I couldn't blame her for being confident.

We continued to sit quietly, waiting for Tawny to give us the okay to speak again.

Sam sighed heavily.

I tapped my fingers on the table.

Sam looked at me pointedly.

I shrugged.

She sighed again.

I closed my eyes and rubbed them.

Finally, Tawny opened her eyes and smiled.

"I caught some of what she was saying," she beamed. "She was telling her sister to stop it. She said something about knowing what she was up to and that she better stop."

If the spirit of her sister was here and Gladys knew it, it would make sense. Maybe she was still bothering her.

Spirits could be mean like that. If they were hateful in life, they were likely to be hateful in death, too.

"Maybe I should get Joe to check it out?"

Tawny nodded. "That might be a good idea. Let's get some more information from Gladys first, though. Make sure she even wants the help. Make sure what we suspect is actually happening."

I nodded. Good advice, as always.

"And we still need to find out about Thomas, too," Samantha added.

I felt a small amount of relief as the nagging feeling in the back of my head began to recede. It was just a matter of time before I could get some answers. And it was a relief to know what questions to ask. After all, if Maybelle's ghost was here, still taunting Gladys after all these years, that would explain a lot about what was going on around here.

I would talk to Gladys tonight after the conference.

The conference was in an old house in downtown Detroit that was built in 1894. We crawled from the car and stood on the sidewalk, marveling at the facade. It was composed of rose-colored granite, with enormous windows and a slate roof.

"Look, Tiffany stained-glass," Samantha gently elbowed me.

"And it has a tower, like the house we're in," Tawny added. Her head tilted so far back I feared she might fall over.

"That's common in the Romanesque Revival style. Come on," Samantha urged us forward.

We entered what Samantha explained was the grand

hall. A white marble fireplace dominated the area. We learned it was only one of the twenty that were in the house.

I eyed the staircase and couldn't help but think how much easier it would be to carry Brodie up that one as opposed to the cramped narrow one at the bed-and-breakfast.

We joined the crowd and checked in for the conference in a large room just off the grand hall.

"This place is perfect," Tawny said. "Do you feel the spirits here? I think they are content. I sense peace."

I agreed. In fact, I was seeing ghosts everywhere, milling around much as we were, trying to figure out what room they were supposed to go to.

Samantha harrumphed.

"Let's focus on the living, if you don't mind. And the house. This could really be an educational trip for you both. There's so much to see and learn about here."

She tripped over a chair because she was staring up at the design on the vaulted ceiling and the tapestries hanging on the walls.

"Where are we supposed to go?" I caught her arm before she walked into another guest.

"Up the stairs," she said. "There's a bar."

As we rounded the corner, Samantha reached out for a pamphlet that sat on an unobtrusive table.

"Ha!" she exclaimed, waving the pamphlet in front of our faces. "A brochure. As good a place to start as any."

We enjoyed several craft cocktails in what was aptly named the Ghost Bar. Samantha was preoccupied with the information in the brochure and only set it down to do further research on her phone. Occasionally she would lift her head to share some fact or interesting aspect of the house.

Tawny and I kept looking around, waiting for something to happen.

"I'm really surprised," Tawny was saying. "Orenda told me this was the place to be. That this conference was the very tiptop of them all. From what I can see," she added, looking around disdainfully, "it's the very tiptop of the riffraff."

"The house has fifty-two rooms!"

Tawny smiled at Sam and continued to scowl at the crowd.

A man beside us had been listening and was quick to motion for the bartender. He asked if we'd like another round. We nodded and made room for him in our little area of the bar.

"Not very impressed are we?" He pulled his stool closer to us.

"Wrong! Very impressed. They say Thomas Edison designed some of the lighting for the house in 1893. Can you imagine?"

I patted Sam's arm as Tawny let the kind man know her thoughts.

"This doesn't seem like it's for the real people. It looks like it's a gimmick for fakes and phonies."

He nodded sagely, and Tawny continued to insult everyone within earshot.

"Let me see what I can do," our mysterious visitor whispered conspiratorially. Then he disappeared before our eyes.

"Well, I missed that," I said, waving my hand where the man had been sitting.

"Sheesh, me too. Where's our heads?"

"I think we're in what used to be one of the bedrooms. The ballroom is over there. Can't go in though," she muttered. "Closed."

We shook our heads at dear Samantha. At least one of us was getting something exciting out of the conference. And it was for the best that she didn't know a ghost was sitting beside her, having a little chat.

The building was remarkable in every way. Tawny and I both felt many spirits, all of them friendly and content. The only disturbing thing was some of the attendees Tawny was complaining about. I didn't blame her. There were several people dressed up in ridiculous costumes. They looked like stereotypical witches, pointy hats and all.

After a light snack and another round of cocktails, we decided to wander around, much to Samantha's delight.

"We have to go to the garden," she said. "It's supposed to be stunning."

We stood to leave, gathering our things, and a distracted Samantha, when a smartly dressed woman called out to us.

"Wait, wait! There's been a mistake!"

We stopped and turned as one.

"I'm so sorry," I murmured.

"We thought they were free," Tawny said.

"Aren't they complementary? For the conference?" Samantha demanded.

The woman stopped short and looked at each of us.

"What?"

"We're sorry. Here, let me pay," I began rummaging in my bag for a credit card. I knew I didn't have the cash for the nine cocktails we'd had between the three of us.

She laughed and put her hand over my arm.

"No, that's not what I meant. I mean, you're in the wrong room. Look at your badges. The room name should be listed at the bottom."

We all looked down at the same time. Samantha and I squinting and digging for reading glasses. Tawny smiled slightly.

"It says 'ballroom' you two. Put your glasses away."

The woman smiled and turned. "Follow me, please."

"It's not closed." Samantha made a strange squeaking sound, then clapped her hands. She seemed to float behind the woman.

We were deposited before two very large decorative doors. A red velvet rope was draped across the front of them and a brass sign above read, "Ballroom."

Our hostess removed the rope and swung the doors open. Then she hustled us in, pulling the doors behind us.

∾

It was breathtaking.

At the end of the ballroom, a large stage hovered a foot above the floor. It drifted through the room as men in tuxedos hurried around, making certain it didn't bump into any tables and had plenty of space to maneuver.

Each table held a two-foot centerpiece of flowers arranged in a cut crystal vase. The flowers changed color every few seconds, shifting among the hues of the rainbow. Light from outside shone through the wall-sized stained glass window and the chandeliers above to glittered and glowed.

A woman amused herself with the light that reflected off the prisms. As the spot of light landed on her table, she tried to catch it, only to sigh wistfully as it danced across the stemware, onto a neighboring table and beyond her reach.

A fountain flowed in the corner next to a tower of champagne flutes balanced precariously one upon the other.

Finally, Samantha focused on something other than the architecture. She whispered, "Be back," and darted towards the fountain.

"Oh, no," Tawny said as we watched her approach the

towering glasses. We needn't have worried. Before she reached out, a glass drifted into the fountain and then into her hand. Quickly followed by two more flutes that did the same. The two extra drinks followed her back to where we stood.

She walked slowly, glancing behind occasionally.

"Look how freaking cool I'm being about all this," she hissed into my ear when she and the floating drinks arrived.

I wondered if she felt as cool as she was acting when she swallowed the entire glass in one long sip.

The man who had bought us drinks earlier was sitting at a nearby table. He caught my eye and held up a glass in a toast. I returned the toast. Apparently, he pulled some ghostly strings for us.

"This is some straight up Hogwarts shit," Tawny mumbled.

She was right. Besides the stunning decorations and the magical touches, we were also surrounded by ghosts. Some were difficult to see, they were more like a thin cloud than a formed being. Some were very much like Joe presents himself to me. I could see them clearly, although it was evident they were not living. They all floated, bobbing and weaving through the crowd.

"It's cold in here. I'm freezing," Samantha murmured. She pulled her sweater around her shoulders and shivered.

I looked at her and then burst out laughing. Tawny did the same.

"What? What's happening? Why are you laughing?"

Behind Samantha stood the ghost of what appeared to be an elderly man. He had a beautiful smile and a calm demeanor. He, too, was laughing. Both of his hands rested on Samantha's shoulders. He pulled one hand off and put his finger to his lips. Then he winked and was gone.

"That's better," Samantha said. She pushed the sleeves

of her sweater up to her elbows. "Now tell me why you were laughing. What's so funny?"

"Should we tell her?" Tawny asked.

"Might as well. She's doing okay with all of this. And our friend there might tease her again."

"Friend? What friend?" Samantha's head was on a swivel. She looked all around the room and then it dawned on her.

"Oh, hell no. Are you telling me there are ghosts in here? Was one on me? Was it touching me? Is it still here?" She was brushing her arms and shaking her hair as though trying to remove spiderwebs.

"He's gone. Let's sit down, drama queen," Tawny said.

Samantha looked at me and widened her eyes emphatically. Then she cut them towards Tawny, who by now was moving towards a table with our names floating above it scripted in glitter.

"Try to be calm," I whispered, taking her arm. "No one is near you. I'll tell you if it happens again, okay? I promise."

That seemed to placate her well enough, and we sat comfortably at our table.

It helped that the moment we sat, a server appeared with another round of drinks and was quickly followed by another who carried plated meals.

"What are we getting?" Tawny asked. "Did you reserve something?"

I shrugged and looked around as discretely as I could. Almost every plate had something different on it, including the three that were placed in front of us.

Tawny had a vegetarian meal, which looked scrumptious even though it was vegetarian.

Samantha wrinkled her nose at the grain bowl but broke into an enormous grin when her medium-rare filet mignon and baked potato appeared before her.

And that meant the lasagna was for me. Always a sucker for sauce, meat, cheese and pasta. I was perfectly content.

As the server pulled away from us, I caught his attention.

"How did you know what each person wanted to eat?"

He smiled a condescending smile and shook his head slightly.

"This is your first time here, then?"

"Yes." I wasn't appreciating his attitude.

"Madame knows what everyone wants to eat. There's no need to bother anyone with mundane questions like that. Enjoy your time here."

Then, seeing my frown and confusion, he bent over and whispered close to my ear.

"There are a lot of things here that will surprise even you. But don't worry. You'll figure it all out soon and really, the people here are very nice and helpful."

Then he sauntered away, presumably to the kitchen to pick up another set of meals. Although it was just as likely, he entered the kitchen and held out his hands while food magically appeared in front of him. Were they even cooking back there?

My thoughts were interrupted when a tiny woman, wearing a black and white hounds tooth jacket over a black pencil skirt with high-heeled boots took the stage. I assumed she was the announcer who would tell us about our speaker for the afternoon.

We all leaned forward with anticipation. Finally, something that was useful to us. After the travel and the drama with Gladys, this trip was paying off.

CHAPTER 7

I was immersed in what Madame was saying, so it took a moment to register that my phone was ringing. I used the 'old phone' ringtone for the kids, so it was sure to grab my attention whenever they called. While I was digging frantically through my bag, Tawny put her finger to her lips and widened her eyes at me. I swear I'm going to break that finger off one of these days.

I finally found the phone and saw it was Peyton.

"Gotta take it," I whispered.

Everyone stared at me as I made my way back through the ballroom. I pushed open the doors and scooted to the side, leaning against the wall.

"Peyton? Everything okay?"

"Uh, yeah. Just checking on something. Is Dad with you?"

"Yes. He flew up with us. Let me tell you, that's a story. You're going to die laughing -." She cut me off.

"Mom. If it's not Dad, then something is here."

"What?"

"If Dad is with you, then something else is here. I've had

a feeling ever since I came by last night and I think it might be the ghost from when we were kids. Not sure though."

"Honey, don't play around with that. No matter who or what you think it is. Leave the house and stay away until I get back. It could be dangerous."

My thoughts flashed back to two events that had never fully been settled. First, both of my children reported seeing multiple ghosts in the house when they were young. Who or what were they?

And, second, twice, I was in a bit of a pickle in the house. Once, when an unscrupulous developer tried to railroad me into selling to him and the other time, when a jerk I went on a blind date with tried to harm me. Both times, both men said something threatened them. They were both scared and left my house screaming like their hair was on fire.

We all assumed it was Joe, protecting me even before I knew he was there. But when I asked him about it, he swore it wasn't him. He even became concerned himself, wondering what else was in the house.

He had done a few 'sweeps' and announced there was nothing there. Still, those events were very clear, and both men had no reason to lie. In fact, it was almost impossible they could create the same story.

I'd put both instances out of my mind, but now, with my youngest in potential danger, all I wanted to do was leave and get home as soon as possible.

"Peyton, please leave," I begged her again. "We don't know what that is. It could hurt you."

"I hear ya, mom. But no, I'm not leaving. I'm calling Hannah and having her come spend the night, too. We'll figure this out before you get home. I promise you, 'This house is clean.'" She added in a creepy, high-pitched voice.

"Not funny," I said. Movies about poltergeists were anything but amusing. In fact, they were actually more accurate than people realize. Samantha's experience with her ghostly visitor touching her shoulder was the type of thing most people experienced. If they knew what made them chill suddenly, they'd likely be horror-struck.

"We'll call you later tonight. How's the conference?"

She was changing the subject and obviously had no intention of following my directions. I sighed.

"It's good. I was pretty obnoxious when I left, so I guess I'd better get back in there. Oh, and I'm turning off my phone for the next few hours."

"Sure thing, mom. Have fun and don't worry."

Peyton hung up before she completed the last word. I'm sure she was trying to disconnect the call before I said something else.

There was nothing left to do now but try to sneak back in as unobtrusively as possible.

It wasn't too difficult. While I'd been outside, the entire program had paused. Not paused as in, they took a break. Paused as in, everyone was frozen in time and space, doing exactly what they were doing before I left the room. Well, everyone except Madame.

I meandered through the tables of people who, moments ago, were in the middle of taking a drink or a bite of food. Some were smiling, some were frowning. Most were seated, and a few were looking in the direction I had gone when I left.

"They knew what was going to happen."

Madame appeared before me.

"I'm so sorry. It was my daughter. We have a ghost and she's there alone."

53

I stammered my excuse and cringed when I heard how it sounded coming out of my mouth.

Madame was gracious. She smiled and said, "Of course. Family first. Always. Find your seat and wait. We'll restart the program in a moment."

She walked away, her tiny short legs working double time to cover the same amount of space. I spotted Tawny and Samantha exactly where I'd left them and made my way back to our table.

Samantha was frozen with her eyes rolled into the back of her head. Tawny must have said or done something to annoy her. Tawny was looking down at her plate, a sly smile played at the corners of her mouth.

I always suspected she was more intelligent than she let on. She did so many things intentionally, just to get under our skin.

Where was my phone? I'd just had it in my hand and turned it off before I came in here. It wasn't in my bag. I looked around the table and checked the floor where I stood.

"We have it. Safe and sound," Madame said from the stage. "I knew you would want to take a picture of your friends. Especially that one," she gestured towards Samantha, who was indeed making a most amusing expression. "No photos, though. We've turned it back on and will let you know if anyone needs you."

I opened my mouth to thank her, but before I could make a sound, she clapped her hands loudly over her head. It sounded like thunder roared throughout the room. I jumped and my hand flew to my heart.

"Are you okay?" Samantha whispered to me.

"Um, yes. Didn't you hear that?"

"No. What did you hear?" Samantha said and looked at

Tawny. She also shook her head, signaling that she had heard nothing.

"Never mind. I'll tell you later."

We listened to Madame talk about the rest of the conference. She talked about the classes and experiences we could take part in. They also encouraged us to bring our familiars along.

Tawny clapped her hands. "Bring Joe! Brodie is your familiar!"

There was no way in hell I was dragging that thing to downtown Detroit and then carrying it through the house and upstairs to this room. I was fairly certain everyone else would have cats or birds, maybe even reptiles, but certainly I would be the only one with a taxidermy beaver that housed my deceased husband.

"He's not really a familiar," I said. "He's staying there."

Tawny pouted but then perked right back up when a panel of ghosts were lead onto the stage for a question-and-answer session.

This was unexpected. And also very intriguing. I did, indeed, have questions.

Later that evening, I told them about what happened when I went outside to take the phone call from Peyton. They looked at me like I'd finally lost my mind. Neither one of them could fully believe me because, for them, nothing had changed. I explained I stepped outside, took the phone call, and when I finished and went back in, everyone was frozen. Everyone except Madame.

"I want to see that," Tawny said. "I'm going to try it tomorrow."

"Me, too," Samantha added.

"You're going to get us kicked out of that place!" I laughed, but inside I was worried. Madame was nice about it, but I could tell she was annoyed. If these two challenged her patience, we were going to be in trouble.

~

Later that night, we sat around the parlor. I'd brought Brodie, and therefore Joe, downstairs. He was bored upstairs and desperately wanted company. He was in the room, listening to us talk and occasionally chiming in with his comments that we steadfastly ignored. We all agreed not to acknowledge him in front of Gladys. None of us was sure how she would take it.

Lex, on the other hand, stared directly at him the entire evening.

"That thing gives me the creeps," Joe said.

"Was Peyton okay when she called?" Samantha asked.

"She called? Why?" Joe jumped into the conversation.

I ignored his question and answered Samantha. He would get his answers at the same time and I would avoid having to explain anything to Gladys.

"She said there was something else in the house," I glanced at Gladys to gage her reaction. "She wanted to make sure all of us were here so she could be sure it wasn't one of us." My lame attempt to convey the fact that Peyton wanted to be sure Joe was with us, while at the same time not mentioning Joe in front of Gladys, was painful. Still, I pressed on. "She's invited Hannah over so they can have a... sleepover."

"Is that a good idea?" Tawny asked. She also knew about our nefarious visitors and agreed that there were plenty of questions to be answered.

"I don't know for sure," I said. "She said she would call me tonight. If she doesn't call in the next few minutes, I'm going to call her."

"Good idea," Joe was nodding his head enthusiastically.

"I'm getting some more wine." Sam stood. "Anyone else?"

We all expressed enthusiastic interest as she left the room with our drink orders. Almost immediately, Lex jumped into the chair she had been sitting in and curled into a tight ball, wallowing in the warmth.

"At least he's not staring at me anymore," Joe grumbled.

Samantha came back with a tray holding two bottles of wine. She poured for everyone and almost sat back down on Lex.

"Oh! Sorry," she said to the cat. She scratched his head, then plopped into a vacant chair that, unbeknownst to her, also held Joe.

No one knew what to say or how to break it to her, but we needn't have worried. Within a second, she screamed and jumped straight up.

"What the hell? You promised, Connie!"

"I didn't have a chance to say anything. I didn't know you were going to sit there!"

"Well, where did you think I was going to sit?" She raised her voice, hands on her hips. "He's laughing at me now, isn't he?"

We all shook our heads and did our best to convince her that Joe was not laughing at her, although it was hard to do. While she couldn't see him as clearly as I could, Tawny could easily see that he was rolling around on the floor, dramatically holding his belly and laughing hysterically.

We both tried our best to ignore him and keep up the charade for Gladys. Samantha had definitely let on that something was going on, but I hoped we could cover for her.

My hopes were dashed when she turned to the empty chair and said, "Joe, you were an ass when you were alive and you're an even bigger ass dead. I'm going to bed."

The room fell silent. Tawny and I looked at Gladys. She was smiling.

"I wasn't sure if she could see him too," she said. "I didn't want to scare her." She turned towards Joe and nodded. "So you're Joe. The one my sister is complaining about."

We laughed uneasily. The fact she could see Joe was a relief, but also a concern. What would that mean for us and our visit?

It didn't seem to make much difference to Gladys, though. She pointed a shaky finger. "It's nothing to laugh about. Be careful with her. She's not as nice as me. In fact, she is evil and wouldn't think of thing of harming any of you. Or all of you. This is something you will have to deal with, you know. You should take my advice now."

I figured this was the perfect opportunity to ask her about her relationship with Maybelle. After the dream last night, I was still shaken and her warnings about her evil sister didn't help.

"What happened between you and Maybelle, Gladys? I know it must be difficult to talk about, but I'd really like to know. Especially if she's still here." I finished by waving my hand around, implying that Maybelle was floating around somewhere in the room.

"She's not 'here' right now," Gladys said, putting air-quotes around the word. "In fact, after she invaded your dreams last night, I gave her what for and I think she's left. At least I hope she has."

"What happened? Why do you hate her so much? And why do you hate Thomas?" I asked.

"Your neighbor said there were rumors that Thomas killed Maybelle. Is that possible? And that you dated him at one time?" Tawny peppered her with questions.

Finally, Gladys nodded her head wearily and stared into the mid-distance. Her eyes glazed over, and she seemed to slip into a trance. Her voice was steady but high and reedy as she told us the story.

"My sister knew my habits very well. I could always feel her watching me closely, learning and studying. Being twins, we were already so similar, but since Thomas and I had gotten engaged, it seemed to have become more intense."

She explained how she and Thomas had become engaged while still in high school and back then, that wasn't as unusual. She talked about how they planned to move into the house and help her parents run the bed-and-breakfast.

"It sounds like a love story." Samantha's voice came from the stairs. She must have decided to stick around after all.

I scooted over and patted the seat next to me. "It's safe," I whispered, and winked at Joe.

Samantha smile gratefully and curled her legs under her as she scooted into the space. When she was settled, Gladys sighed heavily and then continued her story.

～

It was the first day of summer vacation. Gladys threw back the covers and sprang out of bed. She ran to the window and peered across the street. Almost immediately, Thomas's face appeared in his window. He must have been watching for her. She smiled shyly and held her hand up in greeting.

"What are you doing?"

Gladys spun around. Her sister Maybelle stood behind her, hands on hips. "If you don't stop flirting and acting easy with that boy, I'll tell Mother and Father. If they have any sense, they'll put the kibosh on your little party."

"If I'm having a party, then you're the party pooper," Gladys smiled at her joke. "Anyways, Mother and Father already know all about Thomas. And they approve of us going steady."

Maybelle harrumphed and stomped from the room.

Unperturbed, Gladys drifted towards the bathroom. She splashed water on her face and brushed her teeth, and then she chose her outfit for the day. A pink blouse with a cardigan and her best pink skirt. She pulled her hair into a ponytail, then wrapped her hair around her fingers to create ringlets down the sides of her face. The final touch was a pink headband.

Gladys bounced up and down in front of the mirror. She smiled as her ponytail swished back and forth. She pinched her cheeks till they were rosy, then she skipped down the steep wooden steps. When she finally reached the sitting room, she was pleased to see Thomas already there waiting for her. He sipped a glass of water while her mom fussed around him.

"What are the plans for today?" Her mother asked when Gladys swung around the bannister and faced them both.

Thomas smoothed the front of his pants, adjusted his tie, and smiled at Gladys.

"I thought we'd take a stroll. If you'd like to, that is?" Gladys smiled shyly and nodded.

When they were alone on the sidewalk, he turned to her. "You look like a pretty pink princess." He kissed her cheek. She was certain she blushed for the next three blocks.

Shortly after they left, Maybelle stomped down the stairs.

"Maybelle, you sound like a herd of elephants."

"I can't believe you're letting her see him. You know she's getting a bad reputation."

"Now Maybelle, don't be jealous. You can't force someone to like you. It's not Gladys's fault that Thomas likes her. And it's especially not her fault that he likes her more than you. Try not to be hurt darling, you're very special as well."

Mother meandered through the room, fluffing pillows and brushing away nonexistent dust. She repeated, "very special," under her breath before she flitted towards the kitchen. Her focus shifted to a nonexistent stain on the countertop.

Her offhanded comment left Maybelle stewing. She went to the large picture window and squinted through the glass. The foolish couple were almost at the end of the block. Still, she could see that they held hands. And she could see Gladys's stupid pony-tail swinging back and forth.

Summer continued much as that first day went. Gladys and Thomas spent more and more time together. Maybelle spent more and more time sitting by herself, fuming as her jealousy grew. One afternoon, Gladys burst into the house.

"Mother! Mother, come quick!"

"Oh my goodness, what is all this noise for?"

"Look Mother! Look what Thomas gave me."

Gladys held up her left hand. On it, a small diamond glittered.
"Oh! What does this mean?"

"Thomas talked to Father yesterday and neither of them said anything to anyone. Can you believe they kept that secret? But Thomas asked Father if he could marry me after graduation, of course. What do you think, Mother?"

"Why, I think that's just wonderful! Congratulations!"

Maybelle observed the celebration from across the room. When Gladys held up the hand with the diamond, she sprang from her chair.

"Let me see that," she said, snatching Gladys's hand and holding it as close to her eye as possible. She squinted.

"It's so tiny. I can hardly see it."

"I don't care what size it is. I love it. It's perfect." She smiled at Mother, who nodded along.

"Well, I think it's rather pathetic and small." She dropped Gladys's hand and turned on her heel. "Pathetic. All of you." She spat the words over her shoulder.

"Don't let her spoil your happiness," Mother said, reaching for Gladys. "She'll get over it and eventually she'll be happy for you. I think she's just afraid that she's going to lose her sister."

Gladys nodded, but she knew that was not what Maybelle

was upset about. Maybelle had been jealous of Gladys from the beginning. Throughout their childhood and into their teen years, her jealousy only grew deeper and stronger. Gladys said nothing, instead she tolerated the hatefulness knowing one day she would be free of her sister.

She didn't want to upset her parents by telling them how Maybelle was. Plus, it would not have done any good. Maybelle lied. She lied all the time, and she was very convincing. The few times Gladys tried to explain that her sister had done something horrible, Maybelle spun a dizzying story. It was as though she created an elaborate spider web and everyone involved became trapped in it. By the time she finished spinning the lies, Gladys questioned herself, thinking she misunderstood, and Maybelle must have been right.

While Gladys and Thomas spent a year preparing not just to graduate from high school, but also to get married, Maybelle spent a year sulking and plotting.

It was even worse when their parents announced they would turn the house into a bed-and-breakfast for the express purpose of providing a home and a job for Gladys and Thomas. Thomas would take classes at the college while Gladys readied the place for the guests, and they would run it together.

Maybelle wondered where she fit into this whole situation. All these wonderful plans were being made for her sister while she was being left out. It seemed everyone was waiting for her to get out of their way so they could go on with their lives.

While that may have been what they wanted, it was not what Maybelle planned. She was determined to get what she was due, no matter what. She was tired of living her life in Gladys's shadow. It was her turn to shine.

She spent her days thinking and listening. And watching her sister.

A month before the wedding, Maybelle finally had her solution. She woke up one morning and snuck into Gladys's closet *where she found a pink skirt and Gladys's cardigan with the pearl buttons. She pulled her hair into a ponytail and tried her best to create ringlets around her face. Not exactly, but close enough. She smiled at herself in the mirror, satisfied she could pass as Gladys.*

~

"She was dressing up like you?"

"What happened? What did she do?"

We all had questions, but Gladys wasn't saying anything else.

"That's all for tonight," she said. Then she looked at me. "How old are your children? I know the older one is getting married. How about the other one?"

"Well," I began answering her questions although I still had several very pressing questions myself. "Peyton is amazing. She has had a tough road, but she's managed it with grace and confidence."

Gladys looked at me curiously. After her reaction to Hannah being engaged to a Black man, I worried about telling her that Peyton was born a male and was transitioning to female. If a mixed-race couple sent her over the edge, what was this going to do to her?

Still, she asked, and I wasn't ashamed. I told her about Peyton, how proud of her I was and how she and her sister were both exploring their own gifts and abilities.

Gladys looked briefly uncomfortable, then she took a deep breath, literally counting one to four on the in breath and one to four on the out. Then she smiled at me.

"That's nice, dear." She stood and gathered Lex into her arms. The cat growled and tried to get away from her, but she held tight.

Then she stopped and turned back to me. "I'd like to talk to you tomorrow. I'd like to have your help, all of your help,

63

with getting rid of the ghost of my sister. She doesn't bother you, but she terrorizes me every single night. I could live out the rest of my years in peace if I weren't being haunted by Maybelle."

We nodded our agreement, and Tawny spoke up. "I think we can help you with that, Gladys. It's sort of our specialty."

"From what I've seen in my dreams, she was pretty awful. We can help you find some peace, I'm sure of it," I added.

"Good night, then. And you should do it quickly. Tomorrow. No later. I mean it."

Before any of us could ask why the next day was so critical, she was gone.

"What did she mean by that?" Tawny asked.

"Which part?" Samantha said. "She said a lot of strange things."

"First, I'd like to know what she meant by 'do it quickly' and 'no later, I mean it.' Rude, right?" Tawny poured more wine for each of us.

"I'd also like to know what she meant about Joe bothering her sister? Have you seen her? Are you making things worse somehow?" I asked. I shared Tawny's questions, but also had a few of my own.

Now it was Joe's turn to look confused. He shook his head and confirmed that the only time he saw her was the same night I did when I walked into my room. "I've never spoken to her. Well, correct that. I have spoken to her, but she hasn't spoken to me. I don't know how I could be bothering her."

"Well, obviously you're doing something."

Joe gave me a look of frustration.

"You're always blaming me for everything. Sometimes it's not me, you know?"

He did his Jeannie swirl and disappeared into Brodie. I didn't see him any more that night.

"You need to stop doing that." Tawny said mildly.

"I beg your pardon? Stop what, exactly?"

"Being so dismissive of Joe. I know you guys have your issues or whatever, but we need him. There's something going on here and if you keep blaming him for it all, because it's not his fault, you know, then he's not going to want to help and we're going to be screwed."

Samantha was watching us, her head moving back and forth as we talked.

"What did I miss? What happened?"

"Nothing," I said. "Tawny is talking about things she doesn't understand." I was finished with all of this. How dare she talk to me like that? Chiding me for how I spoke to my husband.

"Things I don't understand. Hello pot, it's the kettle...," she muttered.

I did a Gladys impression and turned on my heel in a huff.

"Good night," I flung the words over my shoulder as I stomped upstairs. I was leaving Brodie, Joe, downstairs. I wanted to be alone.

I paused halfway up the stairs, though, when I heard Tawny.

"So what do you think, Joe? Between you and me without the drama, have you heard anything? Seen anything?"

"Not clearly. I know Maybelle is here. I've seen her. And despite what Connie thinks, I have not been bothering her."

"I know. You don't have to explain to me. I am on your side." Tawny said the last part with an emphasis on the word 'I', as though she was the only one who cared about him. Even Samantha didn't stick up for me or say anything. I stood still, just out of sight, with one foot on the next step, and listened intently.

"What I want to know, and didn't have time to ask, is how does Gladys have so many details about what Maybelle did if she wasn't there? Was she spying on her?" Samantha's voice was low.

"Well, maybe Maybelle told her everything. We still haven't heard the entire story."

"That's a good point and I agree. Hang on a second, okay? Let's take care of these." Tawny added.

I heard glasses tinkling and plates being stacked.

"Be right back, Joe," Samantha said. "We'll finish this in a second."

I took the opportunity and darted back down the stairs. Joe looked surprised, but I ignored him and picked up Brodie. I carried the taxidermy beaver back up the stairs as quickly as I could, still not looking at or speaking to Joe. He had no choice but to follow, and as soon as I set Brodie down in my room, sweating and tired from hurrying up the two flights of stairs, I turned to him. I was ready to have it out once and for all.

He misunderstood. No one cared as much as I did. How could they presume otherwise? I had every right to be angry and upset. I was the one whose husband died and was grieving, even though it didn't look like it. They all needed to back the hell off and give me a break. Wasn't I allowed to be emotional? Why did I always have to be the voice of reason and logic?

But before I could catch my breath and say any of these things, Joe's form caught up, blurred, and then became one with the beaver.

I swallowed all the things that were on the tip of my tongue and went to bed.

CHAPTER 8

*T*he next morning I awoke with cat hair stuck to my lips. Lex was standing over me, his claws digging into my chest, scratching his face on mine.

"Gross, Lex! What are you doing up here?" I asked, prying him from my nightgown and rolling slightly to get the twenty-pound cat off of me.

His large green eyes stayed focused on mine as he slide beside me. Then, slowly, he turned his gaze to the left. Not really wanting to, but knowing I had to, I turned my head to look where he was now staring.

There, in the corner of the room, hovered the shadowy form of what used to be Gladys.

"Oh, Gladys! What happened?"

I sat up quickly and looked around for some sign of what I should do. Presumably her body was still downstairs, possibly still in her bed. But if her spirit was here, then she was definitely deceased. It felt strange not to rush to her and try to revive her. Maybe CPR or something would help. Or should I call 911?

As all these thoughts raced through my mind, Gladys continued to float around the room. She was obviously distraught, wringing her see-through hands in front of her see-through body, opening and closing her mouth while no sounds came out.

"Hold on. I got you." I looked at Brodie. "Joe? Are you there? Can you help?"

He did his Jeannie from her bottle act. Still angry from the night before, he glanced my way with a dirty look. Then all of his attention went to Gladys.

After a few moments of conversation that I couldn't hear, he turned to me.

"She said this happened way too soon and we need to help her get rid of Maybelle. We should have done it yesterday. Oh, and she wants you to take care of the cat," he said.

"Right, well, we can talk about removing Maybelle, sure. But, no, I don't want a cat. I'm not set up for it." I glanced at Lex. "Surely someone else-,"

"She said to take care of the cat here and do it at the same time you get rid of Maybelle. Then take over the house."

I sputtered.

"This house? Here? In Michigan?"

The two ghosts rolled their eyes at me.

"Duh," was Joe's eloquent response.

"But what happened? How did she die? She seemed fine last night."

They shared a few more words and Joe, still scowling, told me the rest.

"Gladys has been waiting for you. She needed you here before she could move on. And now that you're here..., what? Wait."

Joe held up a finger and turned back to Gladys. They spoke again, and I still couldn't hear anything. After a few more moments, he looked back at me.

"She wasn't ready to die and she's pretty angry about it.

She's blaming Maybelle, although it's not clear to me how she's responsible. Still, she wants you to get rid of Maybelle and -," Joe turned back to Gladys for a second. "Oh, got it. She wanted you to get rid of Maybelle before she died. That's why she said you should have done it yesterday. It's going to be harder now that she's dead too but, you have to do it. Then take over the house and get rid of Lex."

"She just met me. Gladys, I think you might be confused."

The spirit of Gladys shook her head angrily at me and glowered. Then she disappeared through the wall.

"Joe? What the hell?"

"How should I know?" he asked. "I'm just trying not to bother anyone."

I sighed. I would need to make this right, and soon. Joe was proving yet again to be critical, and I needed him. She said it all wrong, but Tawny was right.

"Joe, wait. Thank you for helping. And, I'm sorry. About everything."

He paused and seemed to think. Then he nodded and turned back.

"Thanks for that, but I think there's something else that's more urgent," he paused again. "Something is wrong."

"Wrong? How?"

He shrugged and faced Brodie.

"She didn't mean, "take care of" as in, care for Lex. She meant to get rid of him. And to make matters even worse, I don't think that was really Gladys."

This was entirely too much ghost first thing in the morning. I needed human interaction, and I needed coffee. Picking my way down the stairs with Lex darting between my legs, I finally made it to the kitchen, where I found Samantha and Tawny. Sam was making coffee while Tawny scrolled through her phone. I'm sure I looked a sight and Sam dropped everything as soon as she saw me. She came to my side.

"Connie, what is wrong? What happened?"

I shook my head, uncertain how to answer her questions.

"I had terrible news," I stammered. "I don't even know how to tell you this. It looks like Gladys died last night."

"What!" Tawny dropped her phone and her head snapped up.

I simply shook my head and shrugged. What was I supposed to say? I had no more information than either of them did.

"Where is she?" Samantha asked. "Hospital?"

"Don't think so. Her ghost visited me first thing this morning. I assume she's in the house somewhere."

"You've got to be kidding me." Samantha said with indignation. "So you haven't even seen her body? Don't you think that's the first thing we should do?"

I nodded. Yes, she was right. We needed to find the body and we needed to call an ambulance. Both things were high on the list of priorities, as was the coffee I still didn't have.

"Okay, this is what we're going to do," Samantha said, taking charge. "First things first. I'm going to call an ambulance. Then we need to find her body. I know you saw her ghost. But we need to actually find her." She said, while handing me a mug and the coffeepot.

Tawny nodded. "I'll be in charge of that," she said. "She's probably still in her bed."

I nodded numbly. Tears of relief poked my eyeballs. I was relieved to have help, and I was relieved to have coffee.

With nothing else to add, I sat in the chair Tawny held out for me.

"What does Joe say about all of this? Have you talked to him this morning?" She asked, scooting me in closer to the table.

I nodded. "Yes, I spoke to him. He was there when Gladys came to visit me."

"And?"

"He said Gladys wants us to get rid of Maybelle's ghost and-." My voice cracked as the rest of the request sank in a little more. "She wants me to get rid of Lex, too. I think she means kill him." At that, the floodgates opened and tears streamed down my face. "I can't. I'd never! Why would she ask that?"

The words kept coming out in stutters and fits. There was no way in hell I would ever hurt an animal. And sure, maybe Maybelle wasn't the nicest person towards Gladys when she was alive, but she had done nothing to me. Gladys was going to need to be a lot more convincing if she wanted me to remove Maybelle's ghost, especially now.

Samantha nodded. "Okay. Okay," she bent down and hugged me. Tawny stuck a tissue in front of me on the table.

"We're not going to worry about any of that now. First things first. You sit here and try to relax a little. Tawny, go find Gladys."

With Tawny on her mission and me blowing my nose, Samantha picked up the phone and called an ambulance.

I said nothing about Gladys wanting me to take over the house. I didn't know what she meant by that, and she wasn't talking. My plan was to ignore it and hope it went away, much like the check engine light on a car dashboard.

～

Tawny found Gladys's body lying peacefully on her bed. She had indeed passed in the night without incident. The paramedics said on first evaluation it looked as though she had a heart attack and went in her sleep.

The paramedics' efficiency and professionalism helped my state of mind and by the time they were ready to leave, I was coherent and composed.

"I hate to ask, but what are we going to do today?" Tawny said. She stood with her phone ready, her thumb poised over the keys.

It was the last day of the conference. None of us wanted to miss it, but considering what happened, all three of us hesitated.

"What time is it?"

I glanced at my watch. "Almost eight."

"I feel like we've already had one hell of a day," Samantha mused.

"Yeah, but what would we do otherwise? Sit around here?" Tawny made a valid point.

We continued to stand in the hallway, none of us sure of what to do.

As the gurney with the covered body of Gladys was wheeled past, I followed it onto the porch and then down the front steps. I watched her being loaded into the back of the silent ambulance. Thomas came out of his house and stood on the sidewalk, also watching.

I waved tentatively.

He smiled and crossed the street.

"So the old battle ax finally kicked the bucket?"

"Well, I don't know that I would put it quite like that, but yes. Gladys died last night in her sleep. Peacefully," I added.

Thomas shrugged. "Peacefully?" He spat the words out. "There was nothing peaceful about that woman. Good riddance," he muttered and turned back to his house.

The ambulance pulled away, and I joined Tawny and Samantha on the porch.

"What did Thomas say?" Samantha asked.

"He said it was good riddance."

Tawny pulled on her jacket and looked at us in anticipation. "We knew he was a jerk. Forget him. Are we going to go today or not?"

Samantha nodded slowly and looked at me. I shrugged and nodded as well.

"We might as well go on and go," Samantha added. "That's the purpose. That's what we're here for, anyway. Let's take full advantage of all the time that we have. Besides, like Tawny said, there's nothing else for us to do here. I suppose there will be an attorney, or I don't know, a family member?"

"She ran off all of her family." Reba the burlesque dancer swayed slightly in her walker. "I hurried over when I saw the ambulance. So, it was Gladys, huh?"

"Yeah, heart attack, they think," Tawny said.

"Can you take care of this?" I asked Reba. "Do you have any idea who to contact? Anyone who could take over right now?"

Reba shook her head, and then she smiled slightly. "I suspect it won't be long now and you'll know exactly what to do." She smartly executed a three-point turn and began working her way back to her own home.

"What the hell is that supposed to mean?" I asked her disappearing back as Samantha and Tawny shook their heads.

"Let's just go. I'm tired of hanging around here." As usual, Tawny got straight to the root of the problem, and I followed her lead.

We dressed quickly. I fed Lex and confirmed everything was locked up before we climbed into the car. It felt right to be going to the last day of the conference. After what we had already missed earlier in the week, none of us wanted to miss even one more minute of the magic that was going on in that building. Even Samantha was feeling how special it was and had confessed that she was sensing some of the spirits that surrounded her.

When we pulled up in front of the venue, Madame was waiting for us and rushed to the car.

"Oh, my dears," she said. "I heard, I heard. I'm so sorry. Sooner than expected, but this is a good thing. It is time for the change. You'll do just fine."

She said that last part, looking at me and patting my shoulder.

That was the second person today to tell me I was going to do fine, but no one bothered to tell me what I was going to do. What did they know I didn't?

We followed Madame into the building and up the staircase. The ballroom doors were open, and we strolled in with newfound confidence. Even Samantha seemed relaxed and more comfortable.

She leaned in and whispered, "I'll go first. Right after they start, I'll get a call. Then you go after lunch. We'll spread it out, so it's not as obvious."

Tawny nodded along, agreeing with Sam's plan.

I cringed. Despite all the drama of the morning, they still planned to answer their phones and make the conference freeze.

Luckily, a large man dressed immaculately in a black tuxedo appeared beside us. He carried a silver tray in one hand.

"Your cell phone, miss." He held the tray in front of Tawny.

"What? Who? Me?" she stammered.

Samantha smiled slyly. "Probably for the best Tawny. So you can really concentrate."

"Fine." Tawny plopped her phone onto the tray. "Here ya' go, Lurch."

I was mortified she said that, while at the same time, impressed she knew the reference.

"And ladies?"

Lurch turned to Samantha and me. He tapped his foot impatiently as we scrambled through our bags for our phones.

We gently set them on the tray. Samantha smiled sheepishly while I avoided eye contact.

"Enjoy the conference," he said before striding away with our phones.

Feeling a bit deflated from the admonishment, we found our table and huddled together.

"Well, that was embarrassing," Sam said.

"I know, right? Like were children or something. Reminds me of them taking our phones up in high school. Remember that?"

"Um, no. We didn't have phones in high school. Was the cell phone even invented then?" Sam asked me.

"Yeah, but not for the average person. Remember the brick?"

We reminisced about the dark ages while Tawny went through phone withdrawal.

After shaking off the awkwardness with Lurch, we focused on the problem at hand.

Turning serious, Samantha voiced what we were all thinking.

"Now what? After today, what happens?"

"I have no idea." I dropped my head into my hands and stared at the table in front of me. I really didn't know.

"Let's just focus on today and see how things go from here," Tawny suggested. "When we get back this afternoon, we'll see how everything stands. Who knows? Maybe somebody will have shown up by now, and maybe a family member or I guess an attorney, or someone like that, will help us. I mean, we can't just leave, right? And what about Lex?" Tawny asked.

She was truly a special person. Concerned about the cat she didn't like, despite everything else that was going on.

"Hey, Tawny, about last night. I'm sorry."

"No, I'm sorry. I never should have spoken to you like that. It's your husband, your marriage, and your situation. I can't relate and it was wrong for me to accuse you when I have no actual idea what's happening."

"Thank you for that. And I am sorry I stomped off mad."

"And came back down to whisk Joe away," Samantha added with a wink.

"No, nothing to wink about. He's furious with me," I added.

"It'll work out," Samantha said, reaching for my hand. "Try to focus on today, like Tawny said. Let your mind relax. We have time and resources to work through all of this later."

Tawny nodded her agreement, and we all settled back into our seats as the program began.

As several guest speakers introduced their familiars and exhibited their special gifts and abilities, Tawny kept looking at me out of the corner of her eye.

"What?"

"I really wish you had brought Brodie the Beaver. Really, Connie, he is your familiar whether or not you accept it."

"No, actually, I think her familiar is gonna be Lex."

I looked at Samantha with my mouth open.

"What? Lex? There's no way he'll be my familiar. In fact, you forget that I'm not even a witch."

"I can't explain it," Samantha continued. "But I know it. You both say that all the time. Well, now I'm saying it. I can't tell you how or why, but I know it."

"Huh," was all I managed. In reality, all I wanted to do was get back home to Charleston and check on Peyton and Hannah. I tried to call last night, but got no answer from either of them. I planned to try calling again this morning, but the events of the day overrode my good intentions. Now, my phone had been commandeered by a butler with a silver tray and a possible grudge.

I was losing what little concentration I had left and immediately my mind switched to mom mode. I worried and fumed as I wondered what those two were getting into and if they were safe. There was most definitely an unknown entity that was hanging out in the house. It was quiet and harmless while I was there, at least towards me, but now it seemed to be getting active. I wanted to know if it was what the girls saw when they were young, and if not, then what was it? It was even worse because Joe had the same questions and concerns. Of all of us, you'd think he would be the one with answers. While I felt like the spirit was protective, the way it protected was unsettling. It had threatened people with harm and even death, all in the name of protecting me.

I barely registered the rest of the conference. The speakers blurred together, and the meal was tasteless. My mind darted from one worry to another the entire day. Only when fireworks began exploding in the conference room, sending bright streaking lights in all directions around us, did I feel the fog lift.

"This is some real Harry Potter shit," Samantha muttered. "I said it before and I'll say it again. Hogwarts. We are at Hogwarts."

Immediately after the fireworks ended in a barrage of sound and lights, another tall, imposing man in a tuxedo appeared.

"Come with me," he said.

We were sufficiently intimidated and did as told.

He hustled us to a waiting car where another tuxedo-clad Lurch was holding the door open.

We climbed in, then he handed us our phones.

"Madame says you have a lot to take care of and need to get back to the house immediately."

"She also said do not hesitate to contact her when you need her," Lurch number two said.

I opened my mouth to ask what he meant, but he slammed the door closed before I could form a coherent word.

I widened my eyes and shrugged in response to the looks from Tawny and Samantha. It's not like I knew anything.

As the car pulled away, I hit the buttons for Peyton and listened as her phone rang and then went to voicemail. I disconnected and tried Hannah. The same thing happened. I debated sending a guilt-inducing text message to both of them, reminding them I was their long-suffering mother who deserved better.

But I didn't.

They were adults. They knew what to do and who to call if they needed help. And I had plenty of my own problems to deal with. Madame was correct. I did not know what was awaiting me and there was a lot to take care of. I decided to reserve my strength for what faced me right now and trust that the kids would do the same. I was wasting energy trying to force them to do what I thought they should do.

The car wound along the tree-lined roads in the sleepy neighborhood. I laid my head back and closed my eyes. This was certainly a new way of thinking for me. Was I becoming more humble? More trusting? So much happened and so much changed over the past year. I was a new person. Thirty something years of boredom followed by a year of upheaval and new experiences convinced me I needed to find a middle ground between the two. This was an opportunity to reinvent myself.

Maybe moving wasn't such a bad idea. I needed to address what Gladys said about me taking the house. Was she serious? What would that even look like? I mean, how often does a house land in your lap? I'd be foolish not to at least find out more about what Gladys meant.

As we approached the bed-and-breakfast, Tawny spoke up.

"Who's that?"

"Who? What are you talking about?" Samantha mumbled.

"On the porch, see him? There's a man sitting there."

I opened my eyes and squinted. Sure enough, there sat a man wearing a dark overcoat and an old Fedora pulled down low on his forehead.

"The 1940s called. They want their hat and coat back."

"Samantha, be nice." I chided. But I had to agree with her. He looked like he had stepped straight out of a noir detective novel.

We got out of the car and made our way to the front porch. When the man saw us, he stood abruptly. He smoothed out his coat and adjusted his hat. He took a few tentative steps towards the edge of the porch and held out his hand. I was first in line and held my hand out as well. As we shook, he asked, "Are you Connie Keyes?"

"Yes, that's me. Can I help you?"

"Yes, actually you can. My name is Stanley Rosenbaum. I am the solicitor for Ms. Gladys Walker. I have her will here. Is there someplace we can talk?"

I nodded dumbly and led him into the house. Tawny and Samantha followed close behind. Everyone introduced themselves and then settled into the drawing room. Lex came out from wherever he had been hiding and did lazy figure eights between my legs. I absentmindedly patted him as he made his way back and forth.

Mr. Rosenbaum smiled mildly at the cat, and then he got down to business. He hauled his old briefcase onto his lap and snapped it open with conviction. After rifling through some pages and papers, he cleared his throat and looked up.

"So I have Ms. Walker's will and testament here and I have notification from the morgue that she indeed passed away and there are no signs of foul play. That makes this the official reading of the will... if you will." He chuckled a little at his joke.

"Let me stop you right there Mr. Rosenbaum," I said. "I'm not sure this is something that we should be hearing. I don't know Gladys. I never met her before we arrived less than a week ago, and I can't imagine there's any reason I would need to know what is in the will. Surely she has family somewhere or even close friends, and this would be more appropriate for them."

Mr. Rosenbaum sat back. "Ms. Keyes, I think there's been a terrible misunderstanding. Not only should you be here listening to this information, this directly affects you in more ways than you realize. Are you not aware of what Ms. Walker did? Of what she left for you?"

"I can't imagine she left anything to me. As I've said, I

didn't know her. She didn't know me. Why would she have left me anything?" I wasn't about to tell him that her ghost told me that very morning that I was to care for the house and exorcise her sister. I didn't even want to think about what she wanted me to do with Lex.

"Well, that is not a question that I can answer. All I can do is tell you what I know and what is in front of me written, signed and notarized by Gladys Walker herself. Please, just let me get through this part and explain to you what information I have and then we can go from there. How does that sound?"

"It sounds like we could all use a drink," Samantha said. She stood and started towards the kitchen. "Wine? Tea? Water? Coffee?"

"Nothing for me thank you," Mr. Rosenbaum said

"Yes, wine," Tawny and I both answered at the same time. We smiled at each other, happily recognizing that we were back on track and thinking the same way again. We sat primly, waiting for Mr. Rosenbaum to continue.

When Samantha came back with an open bottle and three glasses, we all settled down and listened as Mr. Rosenbaum read.

"Ms. Walker came to me about five years ago and told me she wanted to redo her will. Previously, the house was being left to a historical preservation society. And that included all the furnishings and everything else in the house. But when she came to visit me, she was adamant that everything needed to change and be left to one Connie Keyes. And that is you, my dear."

I nodded. "But surely there are other Connie Keyes in the world. Are you sure she meant me?"

"Yes, I'm quite sure. In fact, here is your current address. Charleston, correct?"

I looked at what he was pointing to. That was indeed my

Charleston address. There was no mistake. I was the Connie Keyes that Gladys was referring to. Mr. Rosenbaum added that not only was she leaving the bed-and-breakfast to me, she was also leaving her cat. This I already knew from her announcement that morning. I tried to get some more information from Mr. Rosenbaum. I wanted even more clarification, but he had nothing else to tell me.

"What am I supposed to do with this place?"

"Whatever you want to do with it, I suppose."

"Can I sell it? Can I give it away or donate it? What are the tax implications? What do you think Gladys would've wanted me to do?"

I trailed after Mr. Rosenbaum, dropping my questions bit by bit as he moved towards the door to leave. Finally, he sighed and turned to face me.

"Ms. Keyes, I wish I could answer your questions. Truly, I do. But these are not answers that I have. All I can tell you is what Gladys has in her will and what she has paid me to do. Those are the things that I have done this morning. Paperwork will come through and your signature will be required. After that, it's a fairly simple process. The house will be put into your name and then it's yours. Do whatever you want with it."

I opened the door and Mr. Rosenbaum made his exit, tipping his hat slightly as he walked through the door.

I turned back to face my friends.

"What am I supposed to do now?"

CHAPTER 9

*T*hat evening, Samantha and Tawny packed. They were leaving the next day. I debated between leaving everything and going back with them or staying behind for at least a few days. I needed time to consider all options and think more about the reinvention idea. And I wanted to be alone with my thoughts. Climbing the stairs to my room, though, just about decided for me. If I stayed, I was moving downstairs for sure.

Breathing heavily, I found Lex curled up in the middle of the bed. He was sound asleep and purring. I sat beside him and stroked his long back. He rolled over and stretched. I rubbed his white tummy.

"Don't worry, Lex. You're safe with me, no matter what."

I wouldn't leave him behind even if I had to rent a car and drive him back with me. Tawny suggested the animal shelter. That was a hard no. And I wasn't comfortable taking him on a plane. Especially when I was already juggling Brodie the Beaver.

Speaking of Brodie, and by default, Joe, I wanted to check in with him, too. He didn't exactly have a say in where he ended up, but I wanted to at least give him the courtesy of a conversation about it.

"Hey Joe, are you here? Can we talk?"

I sat in silence for a few seconds, waiting for him to show up. I knew he could hear me. He always could hear me. But whether he was still angry about me fussing at him the night before, I just didn't know.

"Joe, seriously, let's talk. I need to talk."

Within a few seconds, Joe's form materialized in front of me. As usual, he was a little nebulous, but as the seconds ticked away, he became more and more corporeal. I could see him taking form and eventually I could see his face and the details of his expressions. I continued to be amazed by his control the longer he was with me.

"What am I going to do?" I looked at him expectantly. I needed guidance, I needed some direction, and he was the best one to provide that right now.

"I don't know, Connie," he said. "I just don't know. Things are not the way they seem. I keep seeing what I think is the same woman, but they're twins, right? I don't know who I'm talking to. I don't know which one is which. It's confusing."

"Well, that is confusing, Joe, but that's not exactly what I was talking about. I was talking more about the house. What will I do? Do I move here? Do I take over this business? What about the house in Charleston? What about the kids? Oh, my gosh! The kids!"

Forgetting my determination to leave them alone, I picked up the phone and dialed Peyton again. The phone rang and rang and eventually went to a voicemail that was full. I should have known better.

Then I dialed Hannah.

"Hey mom," she answered cheerfully.

"What's going on there? What's happening with the

ghost or whatever? Why haven't you two called me? Is everyone okay? Where's Peyton?"

"Wow, mom. Okay, one question at a time. Sheesh, you'd think we were still teenagers or something."

I bit my tongue and didn't retort with what I wanted to say, which was something like 'then stop acting like teenagers.' But, like I said. I didn't say that.

"Sorry," I said instead. "I'm worried and there's a lot going on here, too."

"I hear ya. Okay, everyone is fine here. The ghost has been behaving. There's been a little activity, but nothing scary. We're still trying to communicate. Peyton is right here. Her phone is dead. We didn't call because there's nothing to tell. What's going on there?"

As I gave Hannah and Peyton, who was listening in, a quick rundown of the events of the last two days, Lex stood and stretched. He sat across from me on the bed and watched me with his head slightly cocked to the side, as though he were listening to the conversation.

"Lex, stop staring," I whispered, and waved at his face.

He continued to look at me, completely unperturbed by my flapping hand. The girls promised to call immediately if anything scary happened or anything changed, and I promised to stop worrying about them because, as they said over and over, there was nothing to worry about.

"Sounds like you have your hands full there, mom," Hannah said. "We're big kids now. We can take care of ourselves."

"Yeah, and we'll let you know if anything happens. My phone is on the charger right now and I promise to keep it charged," Peyton added quickly, before I could say what was on the tip of my tongue.

"Hi to dad," Hannah said.

"Love you both," Peyton added before they hung up.

I looked at Joe and sighed. His smile was comforting, and I knew he felt the same relief I did. Despite our sometimes awkward situation, we always had those kids in common and it would always bring us to the same side.

Lex was still being strange. He opened and closed his mouth several times, all while maintaining disturbingly intense eye contact.

"Are you okay?" I asked him. "Are you choking on something?"

I reached out to grab him and check that he was breathing and swallowing. Before I could, he skittered off the bed and out of the room.

I could have sworn I heard someone mumbling outside my door, but a quick check confirmed it was just the cat.

"Now I'm hearing things," I told Joe. "What is going on here? What am I supposed to do, Joe?"

"I wish I could tell you. I really do. I don't know what the answers are. I know what I would say if I were still alive. But as you're so quick to point out, I'm not. I'm not actually here. I am dead."

I hesitated for several beats. Joe was right. I had been treating him as somewhat disposable, and I wasn't sure why. I guess there was still some residual anger that he left me, even though it wasn't his fault. And now he was with me, but I couldn't actually have him.

"I wish we could've been more like this when you were alive." I swiped a random tear that had trickled out of my eye. Joe nodded solemnly.

"I know. I do too."

I flopped down on the bed, bunched up the pillows underneath my head, and closed my eyes.

If I stayed at the bed-and-breakfast, I would have Joe with me. I doubted he would want to stay in Charleston. And then there was the question of the twins. Gladys recently deceased. Maybelle probably haunting the house, but not causing any problems that I could detect. Gladys demanding I remove Maybelle's ghost. Not to mention the nagging question of why in the world did Gladys leave this place to me? How did she know I would be visiting? Why would she leave it to a stranger?

There were so many unanswered questions and so many things up in the air. I've always believed that when you are overwhelmed with choices and options, the best thing to do is stay still. Give yourself time. Often things will sort themselves out and then it ceases to be overwhelming. You gather your facts and you focus on the decisions you can control. And you allow time for the emotions to settle down.

I decided that was what I was going to do. I would not decide anything right now. I would stay here for a few days at least, get a good night's rest, and then see Tawny and Samantha off in the morning.

After that, I would have the house to myself. It would be quiet and I could sort through some things. I also wanted to get Joe out of his bad mood. I needed to pick his brain, what was left of it, and see if he had any advice for me. Relieved to have a plan, I fell asleep on top of the covers.

That night, I had another strange dream. I was sitting on the porch of the bed-and-breakfast in a rocking chair. My feet were up and I was sipping lemonade. It was very bucolic and idealistic. In the yard were two little girls. One wore all pink and one wore all yellow. They were about seven years old. I watched them play, wondering if they were mine. I soon discovered that they were not, yet I felt responsible for them.

The little girl in yellow was pinching the one in pink.

I yelled at her. "Hey! Stop that! Be nice to your sister."

The little girl looked at me and stuck her tongue out. Then she pinched her sister as hard as she could and ran off in the other direction. The little girl in pink cried. She ran up onto the porch and stood in front of me with big crocodile tears dripping down her face.

"Oh honey, I am so sorry. Let me see." She held her arm out. There was a large bruise already developing just above her elbow. "Maybe some ice will help."

The little girl shook her head.

"Nothing will help. Nothing will help until she goes away."

"That's a terrible thing to say about your sister. Maybe we can make things better. Let's not give up just yet."

"She is so mean. I hate her."

"I understand. She is mean. But we shouldn't hate our sisters, right?"

"She's always mean to me."

In the dream, I got some ice for the little girl, and we sat together on the front porch. I don't remember anything else.

The next morning, I awoke early, shivering on top of the covers. I wandered downstairs, made coffee, and threw a few things together for breakfast. I figured I was the hostess now, so I would send my guests on their way with full tummies. After a little while, Tawny and Samantha were dragging their suitcases and bags down the steps.

"Looks like you made a decision," Samantha commented, eyeing my sweatpants, t-shirt and bare feet.

"Yeah, at least for a little while. I'm staying."

We ate breakfast in silence. Each of us was lost in thought, trying to make sense of the bizarre week we'd just experienced.

"I know what you both are thinking," I broke the silence. "You want to stay here with me and I appreciate that. Really, I do. But you both need to go back. You have your own lives in Charleston, and your jobs, too. Lisabeth needs you at the agency, especially if I'm not there."

"You're right. But after everything, it's hard to leave you."

"Ditto," Tawny added.

We made it easier with their many promises to stay in constant contact. They also promised to come back immediately if I needed anything. Samantha would go to the house to check on Peyton and Hannah, and then report back. She also announced they would get a lecture from Aunt Sam about calling their mom more often. Samantha had been in our lives long enough. She'd earned the privilege to scold the kids.

Tawny said she would contact Orenda and ask for guidance from the spirit world.

"Remember, it's like a social network of sorts. Orenda knows what everyone is up to and she will get to the bottom of it."

I had no doubt.

Finally, the car arrived, and we stood on the porch, hugging and crying.

"I love you guys," I said in a wave of emotion.

"It's not like we'll never see each other again." Samantha sniffed as she pulled tissues from her bag and handed one to each of us.

"I know. It's just a lot, I guess."

"We'll call later tonight. And at least one of us will check on you daily. Take your time with this decision. I agree with Joe that something is still off here, but I can't really put my finger on it. Be careful, okay?" Tawny pulled me in for a long hug, and then she bounced down the steps to the waiting car.

Samantha just shook her head as tears continued to drip from her chin. She pulled me close.

"I got nothing," she sniffed. "I love you. I don't know why I'm crying. I'm ruining my makeup."

I waved as the car holding my best friends and my

support system made its way down the street and finally turned a corner out of sight.

The house was blissfully quiet. I sat in the overstuffed burgundy chair with the high back and arms. It was an enormous chair and was quickly becoming my favorite. As I surveyed my new kingdom, Lex jumped on my lap and settled in comfortably.

I would not make any major choices or decisions, aside from my vehement and unwavering decision that no harm would befall Lex. That was completely out of the question. Instead, I would spend my day taking my time and investigating the house. I wanted to learn more about this place and see if I could find anything out about how and why Gladys had left it to me.

~

It wasn't long before two very loud thumps disturbed my reverie. Lex sprang from my lap as I jumped to my feet.

"What was that?" I asked him. His large green eyes blinked once.

"Never mind, don't answer that," I chuckled to myself. Already I was a crazy cat lady. That took a whole thirty minutes.

I wanted to move my things out of that top bedroom anyway, so I figured I'd combine the two tasks and limit my stair climbing. As I walked down the second-floor hallway, I checked each room. Tawny's was a mess. Bedclothes strewn across the bed, wet towels on the floor, incense ash scattered across the dresser. I made a mental note to ask her who exactly she thought would be cleaning up after her. Samantha's room was pristine. It was as though no one had been in there at all.

More importantly, I saw no indications the thuds had

come from that floor, so I kept climbing. I had my eye on a perfectly pleasant room on the first floor with a bathroom attached. I assume it belonged to Gladys and Maybelle's parents. Gladys had been using yet another room that was obviously added on at some point. The house was really huge. Way too big for one person.

When I reached my room, I shook my head in disbelief. Brodie was on his side, his poor little pinky fingers bent out of shape. The bedclothes were ripped in half down the middle. The pink side was flung over a chair and the yellow side was wadded up in the corner. The thuds apparently came from both dressers being overturned. I was none too happy to see that my own clothes bore the brunt of the turmoil and were also scattered. My underwear and bras hung from the bedposts like indecent Christmas ornaments.

"What happened here?" I scanned the room furiously. "Joe? Are you here? What happened?"

A spark of fear ignited in my gut when Joe didn't answer. I ignored my shaking hands and gathered my clothes and other items, shoving them into the suitcase haphazardly. Then I scooped Brodie into my free arm. Bouncing between the walls of the hallway, I hurried as fast as I could back down both flights of stairs. I left Brodie in the sitting room and flung my suitcase onto the bed in my newly claimed room.

Returning to Brodie, I sat him up and checked him over. As I repositioned his fingers and straightened his shirt and necklace, I whispered, "Joe? You there?"

I heard him before I saw him.

"What?"

"Are you okay?"

"Yeah."

"Can you come out and talk to me? Tell me what happened up there?"

"I guess."

"What's with the attitude?" I asked. "I'm trying to help."

Joe emerged without a glance in my direction and drifted to the chair opposite me. He sat and propped his feet on the coffee table.

If looks could kill, the ghost of my husband would have done me in that very instant.

"Joe? Seriously, what is wrong?"

"Remember talking last night?"

I nodded.

"And you fell asleep in the middle of our conversation?"

I shook my head. "No, I'm sorry. I don't remember. But what happened upstairs? Are you-,"

He cut me off mid-sentence. "There you go. That's why I'm angry. You don't even remember. We were having a pleasant talk, Connie. Talking about how things are now and how they were then. And I had some things to tell you. You know? About what's going on around here. But instead of listening to me. Instead of caring a single bit about what I had to say, you just fell asleep. And then this happened." He emphatically jabbed his finger towards the upstairs.

I was stunned. My first thought was far from gracious. While a million retorts formed in my mind, not the least of which was how many hands would I need if I were to count the number of times he had fallen asleep in the middle of a conversation with me. Or the number of times he was wide awake but still didn't hear me, even when I was saying something important. He had no idea the life I led with him always gone, or always busy, or always doing something that didn't include me. And now, he has the nerve to be angry with me for falling asleep? Especially after the day I had.

Old habits die hard, and I bit my tongue. I don't know why, but I did. My gut reaction, my deeply ingrained instincts, kept me from causing more trouble or risking an argument. It was always easier to just sweep it all under the rug and take the brunt of everything. Just keep the peace.

"I'm sorry," I stuttered. "I'm going to get more coffee."

I walked into the kitchen and closed the door a little harder than needed. Based on what he'd told me before, he couldn't follow me if I didn't leave an open portal for him. I needed a minute to calm down and figure out how to reply to him. We'd gone through the past year, never really talking about our feelings or the changes in our relationship. If that's what you'd even call it now.

"So much for the reinvention and the new Connie," I mumbled as I poured the coffee.

Trying to calm my nerves, I looked around the kitchen.

It was quaint. The walls were painted a sunny yellow color that was slightly faded. The trim was white, as were the table and chairs. Although they were a bit faded and chipped in places. Shabby chic would be the term except they were actually that way because of age, not because of fake distressing in order to achieve the look.

The refrigerator and stove were bright red and freaking adorable. They looked like something from the 1950s but were actually quite modern and high-end. I hadn't really noticed them before, but now, as I looked, I was extremely pleased. This really was a cute place. The kitchen was amazing, and I loved every detail of the old Queen Anne. I saw myself living here and even keeping it open as a bed-and-breakfast.

I shook the daydream away and stood abruptly. This was insane. There was no way I wanted to live almost a thousand miles away from my current home in Charleston. Plus, what about the kids? Was I supposed to just up and leave them? Especially after their father had passed just a little over a year ago?

A little voice in the back of my head reminded me they

didn't need me right there. They were both adults, and they were both moving forward with their own lives, carving their own paths. It would be uncomfortable and strange, for sure, to be this far away, but maybe it was a good thing.

Again, I shook my head. Why was my mind constantly going back to this thought? What was wrong with me? Plus, there were so many questions to ask. I had no idea about the financials and what sort of tax implications there were. Could I even afford to move? And would I sell my house?

I found that I'd been unconsciously pacing back and forth in the kitchen and stopped in front of what looked like an old pantry door. It was the door Gladys had gone through a few days ago. It was flush with the wall and I tried to pry it open. It was still locked.

"Where did she get that key?" I tried to remember what she'd done. She had her back to us, but there were only so many places where it could be.

I opened the closest drawer and picked through paper-clips, rubber bands, takeout menus, a measuring tape, several pens, a screwdriver, and countless other insignificant items. I finally found a single key stuck in the corner of the drawer.

I tried it in the lock and pushed. The door opened.

The creaking and groaning of the old wood told me that this was not a commonly used door. And the smell coming from the basement confirmed that something had probably died down there. Or maybe several somethings.

Despite the smell, this was an investigative day, and my imagination was stoked.

"Joe? I'll be back in a second, okay?" I yelled through the closed door. He didn't reply, which was fine with me.

I was curious to see what was down there and excited to explore a new room.

After five steps, I turned around and bolted back

upstairs. Each step down was darker, smellier, and colder. Michigan had spiders too, and while I was curious, I wasn't that curious.

There had to be a light switch, or even a naked bulb with a pull string, but I did not know where to find either. I rummaged through the drawers in the kitchen again and found an old flashlight. It turned on and then went out immediately. I knocked it against my hand a few times. It flickered and then began to shine.

Armed with my flashlight, but nothing more, I descended the stairs again, confident I would be okay if I could see what was coming. I should have known better.

Of course, the cellar was insanely cold and very dark. It had begun as a crawl space, but in the 1920s, when the economy picked up, people wanted more space for all the things they were buying. So they dug what came to be known in this area as a Michigan basement. The ceiling was low, maybe five feet. I had to duck slightly. A unique problem for my five feet, three inches. I'd never had to duck under a ceiling before in my life.

The floor was compressed dirt, hard and mostly level. There was a roughly ten by ten-foot area that allowed for the five-foot ceiling, which was actually the underside of the first floor. It was composed of exposed wires, pipes and rough hewn wood. The rest of the cellar had a type of shelf all around made of the original dirt. That was the original crawl space. A retainer wall kept that dirt from sliding down into the dug out part.

The crawl space extended far beyond the weak yellowish light from my flashlight. I assumed it went to the edges of the house, or at least close to the edge. It was a space I had zero interest in exploring.

"They have people for that," I muttered.

My senses were tingling and I could feel the presence of one, maybe even two, spirits. I couldn't see anything though, and no one was talking to me. I regretted letting Tawny leave and thought briefly about calling her to come straight back. They were probably still at the airport, waiting to board.

While I could see and talk to the spirits, she still had the better and stronger skills when it came to the unknown.

I thought back to the ghostly panel from the conference and the question-and-answer session. Someone had asked what the best way was to get a reluctant ghost to speak up. The answer was to be patient. The spirit who answered was an old woman wearing a buffalo checked dress and a bonnet. She told about being in a house that she loved until a very loud family showed up. She wasn't violent or angry, so she simply disappeared into the attic and never let them know she was there.

Unfortunately, one night when she was floating around, one of the adults saw her. Of course, they panicked and the very next day, an exorcist showed up. She then corrected herself. No, it wasn't an actual exorcist. But it was someone who was very much like those of us in the audience. She said she knew she was vulnerable. That she could not only be seen but also was feeling a great deal of pressure to talk. She couldn't handle the exposure and sunk even further from communication.

Thankfully, the person who was trying to reach her was patient and kind. Much like Tawny's mother, Orenda, she understood that most spirits just needed a little help, and she was willing to do whatever this spirit needed and wanted.

Eventually, after several days of her sitting around in the

attic, the ghost felt comfortable and willing to talk. As they became friendly, the woman invited the ghost to move into her house, where she continues to live to this day, comfortably and peacefully.

The punchline drew immense applause and cheers because the woman who rescued the ghost was none other than Madame, herself.

From that, I knew I would have to be extremely patient. There was nothing at all that made me think I was going to get answers soon. And I remembered Madame's words that came from one of the Lurches. I could call her if I needed her. I wasn't sure why I would need her or what I might ask of her, but it was still a comfort.

I looked around as much as possible with the weak flashlight and was rewarded when I found a switch on the far wall. I flipped it with fingers crossed. It flickered on briefly and then sputtered out.

Great. I would need to find a replacement bulb, too.

Shining my light on the ceiling, I could see the naked bulb hanging over a small patch of rug. On it sat a small table and two chairs. Old crayons and decaying brown paper, curled at the edges, lay on the top. Next to them sat a bottle of what looked like nail polish. It was ancient. The lid caked closed long ago.

My investigations were over for the moment and I trudged back up the stairs. My right knee was acting up from all the up and down that morning. All I could think was how fitting it would be for me to fall or trip here alone in this house and lay there on the floor of the cellar. My mind continued to reach and in no time, I had myself lying on the floor, the battery in the flashlight going out and no one to help me.

Then I thought about Joe. But even if he could reach me, what could he possibly do? And then the big question. Did he even hear me? How would he even know where I was? The simplest thing was to climb the stairs carefully and then put my cellphone in a pocket. It would always be near me. Just in case.

As I reached the last step, I heard a voice.

"I will make you pay for this. Over and over, I'll make you pay."

I stopped and spun, almost fulfilling the prophecy of my own demise, but I managed to catch myself. I'd only slipped a step or two and nothing was injured. I stood stock still and listened again. There was nothing. No sounds at all and definitely no more voices.

"Hello?" I called down into the darkness. "Who's down there? Gladys?"

No one answered me, which was good and bad. On the one hand, I was a bit relieved. But on the other hand, I was sure I'd heard the voices. Could it have been the spirits I was sensing? Or something else?

It was time to talk to Joe. I hoped he was finished pouting and would be willing to discuss our situation. If I was going to stay here, whether for a long time or just a short while, we needed to be on the same page. I knew I was going to need his help. Added to that, the only people I knew here were Reba the angry burlesque dancer next door and the cranky old guy across the street. Oh, and possibly a ghost or two still hanging around in the basement.

When I returned to the sitting room, that's exactly what Joe was still doing.

Sitting.

And I didn't say a word about it.

We had to work out whatever was going on between us. I sat and looked at him.

He raised his eyes.

"Should we start over?" I asked.

He nodded.

"I'm sorry I yelled. I'm sorry I accused you of being insensitive when you fell asleep. I know it was a rough day." He then added, "And I know I did that to you a million times before."

I smiled with relief.

"I'm sorry too. I should have made an effort to finish our conversation first. I think I've been taking you for granted, and I know I've been insensitive to your situation." I gestured vaguely towards the beaver sitting beside him.

"Did you love me?" he blurted.

"Yes! Of course!" I answered quickly. How could he even ask me that? "I loved you so much."

I stopped talking and paused for a beat. Then added, "I still love you."

Joe's face crumbled. He looked like he was in pain, and I jumped up to move closer to him. I covered his hand with mine. While I couldn't actually feel his hand beneath mine, I could feel the warmth that traveled from my palm through to the back of my hand and up my wrist.

"Can you feel me?" I asked him.

Joe nodded. "Warm," he said.

"Me too."

It surprised me to realize we really hadn't tried to touch since he passed. I was sure it had happened here and there, but nothing deliberate like this. And I definitely hadn't had the feelings I was having right now. I would have remembered it.

I was lost in thought when Joe cleared his throat.

Another thing I found amusing, but prided myself on not commenting. I was really trying to read the room.

"What?"

"We need to talk about what's going on in this house," he said. "But not here. Can you take me outside?"

He drifted to Brodie and disappeared before I said anything. I sighed and lifted the thing into my arms and lugged it through the front door.

I glanced up and down the street and saw Thomas standing on his front walk, watching me. He had his arms crossed over his chest and his head cocked to one side.

"Does he just stand there and stare at the house all the time?" I muttered.

Joe moved out of the beaver and drifted just to my right. "Can he see me?" He asked in a low tone.

"I don't think so," I replied. "But he definitely sees me standing here, talking to myself. Or worse, talking to a stuffed beaver. Are you sure we need to be out here for this?"

"Yes. I don't want anyone inside to overhear us. Come over here. He can't see you behind the shrubs."

I followed Joe and settled into an old wicker chair that had seen better days. Unlike the other furniture that provided a homey welcome to all who visited, this old chair was stuck behind the shrubs, in a corner that rarely, if ever, saw daylight. It was dreary and chilly.

"Okay, what do you want to tell me that can't be overheard?" I asked, trying to get comfortable in the chair. The front of the seat cut into the back of my thighs and my feet went numb. Short people problems are real.

Joe settled next to me, keeping one eye peering over the shrubs to watch Thomas and keeping another eye on me.

"In case he comes over and actually hears you talking to yourself," Joe laughed. "I'll warn you."

"Thanks! That would be awkward!"

"I'll get right to the point. There are two spirits here now. One of them is definitely Maybelle. That's who we both saw the other night. And now that Gladys has passed, she is here too. But the problem is, I can't tell which one is which. And from what we understand, we need to be careful of Maybelle. She's dangerous."

I nodded as he spoke. "Can you tell what they are wearing?" I asked. "Gladys always wore pink, and I've seen pictures of Maybelle in yellow."

"No, and that's another problem. They are both in pink."

"Are you sure?" This surprised me. In every picture throughout the house, the twins were in different colors all the time. There isn't one instance that I could find where they both wore the same color. And don't even get me started on the bedroom. "I got the impression from Gladys that it was a major issue with them. They had their signature colors to tell them apart. Even their parents couldn't tell them apart without the color hints."

Joe nodded. "Shhh! Neighbor coming."

I stood up and peered over the hedge. Sure enough, Thomas was picking his way towards the porch.

"Hello neighbor," he called out in greeting. "Why are you sitting way over there?"

"Oh, I'm just thinking," I said by way of a lame excuse for why I was miserable in an old chair in the dank chill of the corner of the porch.

I stood shaking my legs to get blood flowing again just as Joe swooped back into the beaver. I knew he was being extra cautious. Sometimes people could see things and not realize it. Other times, people would see a spirit for the first time and it didn't always go well. Joe was determined not to be the first spirit someone saw. He just didn't want that responsibility.

"So the old bat is dead, huh?" Thomas said.

"Yup." I had nothing else to add. He was being rude again, and we had already had this conversation.

"And she left the place to you?"

Again, I nodded. "How did you know?"

He didn't answer my question and instead asked another one of his own.

"Have you been in the basement yet?"

I hesitated.

"Ah! You have!" He said. "Find anything interesting?"

"I'm not sure what you're talking about. What would I have found?"

Thomas smiled. "My dear friend, there is so much you don't know. In fact, no one but me knows. I guess it's safe now."

"What don't I know?" I asked.

We both jumped when a loud noise from inside the house rattled the window frames. I turned to see what I thought was Gladys, banging on the window from the inside.

"Ah, Maybelle," Thomas muttered. "Better go see what she wants."

CHAPTER 10

"Maybelle? Or Gladys?" I looked at Thomas. "She's in pink. I thought that was Gladys. How can you tell them apart?"

"The evil radiates from her. Can't you feel it?"

"No. No, I can't."

I followed Thomas into what was feeling more and more like my house. In fact, I was a little offended that he didn't hesitate to open my front door and walk right in as though he owned the place.

I stopped and turned back. I wanted Joe with me. With more than a little effort, I went back and grabbed Brodie by the arm and dragged him behind me.

"We've got to get you something else to bind to," I mumbled as I pulled him across the threshold.

"Is that your husband?" Thomas asked.

I wasn't sure how to respond to that. How did he know? But before I had too much time to think about it, Maybelle or Gladys, or whoever, solved the problem for me.

"Thomas! Get out!" She screeched like a madwoman.

"Whoa, whoa," I tried to be the peacemaker. "Gladys, it's okay. He can't hurt you now."

"I'm not Gladys you ninny. You get out too! You've proven to be useless to me!"

Quick as a flash, Joe's form shot from the beaver and went face to face with the spirit of Maybelle. They swirled around each other for a few seconds, and then Maybelle drifted away. Somewhere in the back of the house, we heard a thud and a crash and then it was silent.

"Are we safe?" I asked Joe.

"For now," he said. "But it won't last long. She's pretty angry. And surprisingly strong," he added.

"What the hell?" I turned on Thomas. "Explain."

"You first," he smiled. "Who's your friend?"

I hadn't found myself in the situation of having to explain Joe and the entire Brodie the Beaver issue many times, so I stumbled over my words. But after a few false starts, I explained to Thomas that when my husband died of a heart attack, his spirit attached to me and followed me home. Then, because the fates are just mean, he ended up attaching to the beaver. Not only was it humiliating for him, but also for me. If I wanted Joe with me, I had to lug the beaver around with me, too.

"That's not so bad," Thomas said. "He looks friendly enough. Stay loose, dude," he chuckled as he imitated the Shaka sign.

I rolled my eyes at Joe. He smiled.

"Okay, so you know who my ghost is. Now tell me who yours is."

Thomas sat down and sighed. "The last time I sat here was when I was eighteen. I had just become engaged to Gladys. We were so young. But we were happy. It was going to be a wonderful life. Then her sister ruined everything. Maybelle, that old witch. I know she killed my pretty pink princess."

"Wait, now you're calling her your pretty pink princess?

The same woman you called an old biddy and battle ax? So now you're all about your love even though she was right here the entire time, and you both were too stubborn to make it right, to talk and fix things."

"Oh dear, that wasn't Gladys."

My blood ran cold. "What do you mean, that wasn't Gladys? Who have I been with all this time?"

"That was Maybelle, pretending to be Gladys. Really, we should go look in the basement. I know that's where she is. Maybelle never allowed me to step foot on the property when she was alive. She would have shot me. It just confirms that Gladys is here, somewhere."

"Okay," I said slowly, trying to process all the information I'd just received. I didn't know what to make of this. Gladys was convincing. She had told stories of her sister and how awful she was. And I guess they were true. Maybelle was the evil one. But I didn't suspect for even a moment that the Gladys I knew was actually Maybelle, pretending to be Gladys. It was confusing.

And added to that, if she was so evil, why in the world did she leave the bed-and-breakfast to me? Even if she wanted me here in order to remove the real Gladys's ghost, she wouldn't have to leave the house to me in order to do that. Surely she would have suspected that I'd be looking into this. Or that Thomas would want answers and come looking for them. What was her plan?

"Tell us what happened. How did all of this start? Gladys, or I guess it was Maybelle, told us about trying to seduce you," I felt myself blush. How annoying. Still, I pressed on. "Was she successful? Is that why all this anger and animosity between sisters? What really happened?"

Thomas sat back in his chair, which was actually my favorite chair, and stretched. Then he began a very intriguing story.

"Yes, she tried, but she failed. I knew all along it was her and not Gladys. It didn't take long before she knew I knew. Maybelle wasn't stupid. She was incredibly gifted with the ability to transform herself into whoever or whatever she needed to be to get what she wanted. I remember every part of her act."

~

Maybelle knew she needed to adjust and do so quickly. Composing herself with a deep breath and then smoothing the front of her sweater, something she'd seen Gladys do many times, she turned and smiled her sweetest smile.

"Darling," she began. "I'm not sure exactly how to say this. I want us to be closer than we've ever been before and I think I know how we can do that."

She was taking a gamble and a chance that the couple had not had sex before and that she could talk him into it before they, actually Thomas and Gladys, were married.

Thomas sat up and turned to face her. His smile was small and smug. Maybelle wanted to slap it off of his face.

"Yes? Dear?"

Instead of striking him, she forced herself to blush. She wasn't sure if she was succeeding, but that was another thing that Gladys did regularly. She blushed at almost anything. And if she knew anything about her sister at all, she just knew this was something that would make her cheeks rosy.

"Well, um, I just think it's time. You know?"

She smiled what she hoped was a sexy and alluring smile. While still trying to appear demure and shy. God, what a mess. How did Gladys live in her mind with all these things she kept up? It had to be exhausting.

"No, I don't know. Tell me."

Thomas was more stupid than she had ever given him credit

for being. He was thick-headed and just dumb. Any other man in the entire world would know what she was talking about by now, but this dolt was still sitting there, smiling like an idiot.

She took a breath and attempted to compose herself.

"I don't want to say." She faked a giggle. "It's too embarrassing."

"What is?"

Maybelle lost all composure this time. She whipped her head around and stared Thomas straight in the eyes.

"Sex. Thomas. I want to have sex. Good grief, how stupid are you?"

And then she covered her mouth with her hand, and fake giggled again. "I'm sorry. It's just so awkward for me. I love you." She hoped that was enough to offset her outburst. If he were anything like a normal man, he would quickly forgive and forget the outburst in exchange for a roll in the hay.

Maybelle waited for what she knew would be an enthusiastic response. And she kept waiting. Finally, after what felt like a full minute had passed, she risked a look in his direction.

Thomas was still looking at her. The smile had disappeared from his face and he looked angry.

"I'm not as stupid as you think, Maybelle."

"What? How could you? What? You think I'm my sister? Thomas! I thought you knew me better!"

Maybelle did her best to appear distraught and offended. She fought hard to hide the fear that suddenly struck her heart as she realized, even as she continued to fake it, that Thomas had figured it out.

"I do know you. And I also know Gladys. And I know you aren't Gladys, Maybelle. What's this all about? Why are you here? Saying these things?"

"Honestly, I never!" Maybelle stood and moved towards the door. She had to get out of here immediately. Now she really was embarrassed and angry that her plan didn't work. She had come to the house fully prepared to sleep with her sister's fiancé and then tell the world what had happened. She was going to tell everyone that he raped her, or maybe not. Maybe she would tell everyone they were secret lovers. Either way, she was determined to compromise him and ruin everything for Gladys. Instead, it looked like the opposite happened and she was the one to be ruined.

Thomas stood and followed her to the door.

"I don't know what you're up to, but I'm telling Gladys," Thomas said. "This isn't right." He held the door open, and Maybelle flounced through it.

"She won't believe you," she said over her shoulder as she hurried away from the greatest embarrassment of her young life.

Thomas returned to the house and found the car keys. He drove straight to the library where he wasn't a bit surprised to find Gladys in the middle of a book that held ten toddlers enthralled. He smiled and waved when she noticed him. She knit her brow together with a questioning look. He smiled and shook his head slightly.

"Nothing's wrong," he conveyed to her. Although that wasn't the case. A lot was wrong.

When she finished reading, she went to him and pulled him into a hug. He glanced down at her left hand and smiled to see the ring there.

"What a wonderful surprise," she said as they pulled back from each other. He only smiled a tight, thin-lipped smile and Gladys pulled a worried face again.

"What? What happened?" She demanded to know.

Thomas led her to a small table in a private corner and told her about his visit that afternoon.

"It wasn't hard to figure out that it wasn't you. Your sister is very, unique." He shrugged at the word. There wasn't another one that he felt comfortable using for the sister of his fiancé. But *while he would not say what he was thinking, he definitely was thinking it.*

Gladys, on the other hand, had no trouble finding the words to convey her feelings on the matter.

"That bitch!"

She blurted and then looked around quickly. No one had overheard her, thankfully. She lowered her voice and leaned in closer to Thomas.

"That bitch," she said again, quieter. "I can't believe the nerve. All my life I've put up with her foolishness, but this is just too much. She's gone way too far this time."

Gladys stood. She smoothed the front of her sweater and then held out her hand for Thomas. "Come on. We're going to put a stop to this once and for all. Right now."

"Now, wait. What are you going to do? Don't be rash." He followed her, struggling to keep up.

"Oh, I'll be rash all right."

When they arrived at the house, Maybelle had changed back into her yellow slacks and a button-up blouse. She was lying on the sofa, reading a book. Actually, she was pretending to read. She had seen Thomas pull out of the driveway twenty minutes ago and had a pretty good idea of where he was going.

When she heard his car pull into the driveway of the bed-and-breakfast, her stomach knotted. Then she reminded herself that she'd done nothing wrong. She simply went to visit the fiancé of her sister and he tried to attack her. Maybelle was going to blame everything on Thomas. It was all his fault. He tried to seduce her and dared to lay his hands on her and...

Her explanation and excuses were cut off when the door banged open and the fury of Gladys stood in the doorway.

"Loud enough?" Maybelle said. She stood and faced her sister.

"What did you do? What were you thinking? How dare you try to sleep with Thomas? And how dare you pretend to be me? That was so low Maybelle. Even for you."

"I've no idea what you're talking about," Maybelle said. She chanced a look at Thomas, who was pressed against the wall of the sitting room, trying to make himself as small as possible.

"Don't give me that shit," Gladys said. "You know exactly what I'm talking about."

Maybelle laughed. This was the first time she'd ever heard her sister curse. It sounded funny coming from her mouth. Her laughter further incensed Gladys.

The years of abuse, tiny pinches all the time, pulled hair, missing jewelry, damaged clothes, and mysterious rumors had finally taken their toll. Gladys had had enough. Thomas was hers, and she wasn't about to let anyone take him away from her. Least of all, Maybelle.

She lunged across the room, hands out in front of her, reaching for Maybelle's neck. At the same time, Thomas yelled, "No!" and moved to reach for her waist.

Maybelle stood rooted to her spot, hardly daring to believe that this was actually happening and that her meek and stupid sister intended to harm her.

Gladys twisted away from Thomas's reach and launched herself onto Maybelle. She began clawing at her face with her nails, pulling her hair and screaming at her the entire time. Maybelle fought back and the young women rolled over each other, banging their heads into the floor and knocking over lamps and other odds and ends.

Thomas rang his hands, uncertain what to do. He knew he needed to stop the fight, but he also knew he didn't want to hurt either of them, especially Gladys. And since Gladys seemed to have the upper hand, he feared she would be the one he might accidentally harm.

He looked through the front window and saw a sight that gave him great relief. It was their mother, coming up the path from the neighbor's house.

He called to her to hurry and come quick.

When she entered the room, she paused and then leapt into action. She raised her voice and ordered the two young women to stop what they were doing immediately. Then she dove into the jumble of arms, legs, and hair and began peeling them off of each other.

When she finally had them separated, each one on one side of her, all of them breathing heavily, she turned to Maybelle.

"What did you do?" She asked.

Maybelle opened and closed her mouth, trying to find the words. It fit that her mother simply assumed she was the instigator in this entire fiasco.

She needn't have worried about coming up with an excuse. Gladys piped up.

"She tried to seduce Thomas!" She exclaimed, pointing a shaking finger at Maybelle. "She dressed like me and tried to trick him!"

Mother turned to Thomas. "Is this true?"

He nodded and then looked away.

Mother didn't say another word. She grabbed Maybelle by the arm and pulled her upstairs to the very top floor of the house. She put her in the room, closed and locked the door.

Maybelle recovered from the shock of having her mother treat her that way. She banged on the door.

"Let me out! I'm sorry! Let me out!"

Mother ignored her and walked away. Maybelle eventually cried herself to sleep.

～

"Wow," I exhaled. "Gladys, who I guess was really Maybelle, never told us anything like that, did she, Joe?"

He shook his head and then added, "And I haven't been able to get anything out of Gladys, the real Gladys whose spirit has been here the whole time we've been here."

"She's been here longer than that," Thomas's voice choked as he spoke. "I know she's here. I've felt it for all these years, but any time I tried to press the issue or get close to finding answers, Maybelle would start up the rumors again. She liked it when people thought I'd had an affair with Maybelle and then killed her. When she pretended to be Gladys, she acted so self-righteous. Everyone was on her side thinking she turned away from me, her fiancé, because she believed so strongly that I'd done something to her sister. She told everyone she could forgive the affair, but not the murder."

"The police, surely?"

"No. No good. She was an excellent actress, as you've seen for yourself this past week. She had everyone convinced. They questioned me, but since there was no body and no proof at all, Maybelle went down as a missing person officially, but everyone else thinks they know the true story."

"Why do you want to go to the cellar? What's down there? What do you expect to find?"

"I expect to find the remains of my beloved," he muttered. I saw him swipe away a tear just before he turned away.

I looked at Joe and frowned. He shared the look as we both felt a pang of sympathy for the old man. After all, he was experiencing what we were, but he had been doing it for decades. My love died too soon, but he lost his tragically early.

CHAPTER 11

*M*aybelle remembered it just as Thomas told it. She was mortified that he knew so much more than she thought he did and slammed the door behind her, pleased to see she could manipulate solid objects now. Her strength was developing quickly, much to her relief. She hated how she appeared to Connie that first time. So weak and pathetic. She learned from watching that Joe character. He was a buffoon, but she learned as much as she could and then, of course, went on to do it better.

They were preparing to go down into the cellar, and she wanted to be ready. She would orchestrate a show that would send all of them running from the house in fear.

Then, they would understand what it was like being her.

She remembered the morning after when everyone panicked. They started looking for her frantically, fearing she had run away or was in danger or harmed.

It amused her, in her disguise as Gladys, to watch the worry and concern on their faces. She felt very special and important until she overheard her parents.

"She's not right in the head. She never has been. I'm worried about her out there. She might hurt someone."

"I know, but there's only so much we can do. We tried for so long. Let the police do their jobs. Maybe they can find her before it gets too bad."

Maybelle remembered sitting on the top step. Not right in the head? Is that what they thought of her? She racked her brain trying to think of how she acted that made them believe that. She couldn't come up with anything. Sure, she made some dubious choices in the past, but there was always a reason. A perfectly logical reason.

Like the rabbit. She truly thought people ate rabbits and that the one her parents bought for her and Gladys was for food. Then there was the cat. Cats always hated her. When it scratched her, she just reacted like any other person would and slung it by the tail into the wall. And as far as how she was with Gladys, that was just sisters teasing. It meant nothing. It's not like the bruises didn't heal. Even what she'd done the night before was easily explained. She didn't want to go away, and they were going to make her leave. All she wanted was to stay with her family. Why was that bad? What made her not right in the head when that was what she wanted? Wasn't that a good thing?

She had to make sure things continued to go well. It was probably best that everyone thought she'd run away. Maybe they wouldn't even go looking for her. No, she had to stop thinking that way. She corrected herself. Maybe they wouldn't even go looking for Maybelle. That would keep people from poking around too much in the basement.

Still, she had wanted to convince Thomas. She failed the day before, miserably, but had no choice but to try again. And if she had no choice, she was going to make sure he didn't either.

She decided to give it her best effort and then, if she could not convince him she was the real Gladys, she would go to the second part of her plan. After all, what could he say? He couldn't prove anything. And he couldn't disprove anything either.

She would accuse him of having an affair with Maybelle and then, as Gladys, she would break it off with him. She might even go so far as to accuse him of killing her poor, dear sister.

But, slow down, she reminded herself. Wait and see how it goes. Maybe he would go along with it all. After all, what was the difference? They looked the same. Couldn't he just pretend?

Dressed in her sister's clothes, Maybelle crossed the street and rapped smartly on the door to Thomas's house.

He opened it immediately.

"I saw the police car. What's going on?" He asked.

"Maybelle ran away."

Thomas immediately stepped away from her.

"Maybelle?"

She nodded. "Yes, that's what I said. Maybelle ran away."

Thomas shook his head yet again. He looked at the young woman.

"I can tell it's you, Maybelle. Where is Gladys? What have you done?"

"I'm sure I don't know what you mean," she said. "See, look. I even have the ring."

She was grateful she'd remembered to take it off her sister's dead finger. It was the one thing she'd forgotten last time.

Still, it didn't seem to convince Thomas. He continued to shake his head, and now his whole body was beginning to shake.

"Where is Gladys?" He asked again. "Tell me now or I'm going over there and tell them all you are really Maybelle."

Maybelle paused at the realization that her plan would not work. She would have to adjust.

"Oh, Thomas. Why can't you make things easier?" She sighed as she brushed past him and made her way into the sitting room. She looked around quickly to ensure they were alone, then she leaned her head close to his and whispered.

"It's unlikely they will believe you. If you say anything at all, I will tell everyone you killed Maybelle. I'll say you did it because you were so angry with her for tricking you. I might even let slip that poor Maybelle told me you forced yourself on her, thinking it was me. Of course, being the wonderful sister that I am, I would have to break up with you. It would be the end of the Gladys and Thomas love story. And most likely, the end of you as well. I'm not sure your reputation could recover from something like that, Thomas."

He listened to her, his mouth hanging open and his heart beating faster and faster.

"Surely your own parents can tell you apart. It'll never work. There's no body. No one would believe you!"

"Are you sure about that?" Maybelle asked coyly. "Are you sure there's no body? Nothing will turn up in a most inconvenient place?"

At this, Thomas stopped talking. She watched as the realization that not only was he being manipulated and bribed by his fiance's sister, but it was dawning on him that Gladys really was gone. Most likely dead based on what Maybelle was telling him. He couldn't believe she would actually do something like that to her own sister.

"How could you, Maybelle?" He asked.

Maybelle smiled and stood. "It was simple, actually. And from now on, I am Gladys. Never call me that other name again. Say anything about this and the police just might find an unfortunate piece of evidence in your house."

"Where is she? Where's her body right now? Doesn't she deserve a funeral? Something for closure?"

"No, Thomas. No, she doesn't."

And Maybelle left the house. From now on, she was Gladys, who wore pink, and who was so devastated by the disappearance of her sister, she simply couldn't be with Thomas any longer.

She planted a carefully constructed rumor that Thomas and Maybelle had been together and it broke her heart. She was standing by her sister, though, and would have nothing more to do with the scoundrel across the street.

She was amazed she'd been able to keep the secret for all those decades. And now it might be ruined because the one person she knew could help, the one person she called to get rid of the ghost of her sister, was turning against her. She was so close. Connie was right where she wanted her, moments away from putting into action the plan that would secure her eternity in her house. Then she went and had a heart attack.

Maybelle was pretty certain it was because of the damn cat. She knew he wasn't really a cat. There was something about him. She'd ignored it for the five years that she'd had him, treating him like a cat and brushing aside the strange things he did. But she also knew he planted ideas in her mind. Ideas like changing the will.

Enough memories. She had to prepare for the show. It was going to be a doozy, and who knew how long it would run for? She had a new plan, and it was time to set it in motion.

∽

We followed Thomas to the cellar door. He knew exactly where to go and pulled a flashlight from his back pocket when he got there.

"Get your own if you've got one," he instructed. "Better to have a backup, just in case."

I nodded and pulled out the flashlight I'd used earlier that day. I shook it until it came on.

"Wait!" I said and rummaged through another cabinet. "Here," I handed a fresh light bulb to Thomas. "It burned out. We can change it."

Thomas nodded and cradled the bulb in his left hand while his right held the flashlight. We picked our way carefully down the stairs. I patted my back pocket, relieved to realize I had remembered to put my cellphone there.

As we went lower, Joe hovered just behind me. He was nervous and wasn't saying a word. In fact, he still hadn't spoken to Thomas or Thomas to him. It's like they knew the other was there, but they were going about their business as though nothing was unusual.

When we finally reached the bottom of the stairs, Thomas switched the bulb to the crook of his arm and held up a fisted hand to stop us.

He turned towards me and put his finger over his mouth. As if I was saying anything. As if I had anything to say. No, I was along for the ride and that was all. There was too much to think about and process for me to have an opinion at this point. I just wanted to see what happened.

Thomas began playing his flashlight over the floor of the cellar. He walked further and further away from me. Then he stopped and placed the light bulb on the ground. He stood and continued sweeping the light across his path as he made his way into the furthest corner of the room and shined the light across the crawl space.

I don't know what he saw, but I heard a loud sob.

The naked, burned out light suddenly came on and we all turned towards the small table in the middle of the room.

Two young women sat there. Arms crossed over their chests, legs stretched out in the same pose.

"I'm sorry they are sending you away," the one in pink said.

"No, you're not. You're happy. Now you have everything for yourself. Thomas, our parents, the house. You've always wanted it all, and you've always had it all."

"How do I have it all? We are twins. We have the same parents, same house, same looks. The only thing I have is Thomas, and you've done your best to take that away from me."

"You're right. I'm sorry." Maybelle sat up and moved closer to Gladys. "I don't want to go away," she whispered. "I'm scared."

"It might be a good thing," Gladys said, her voice softening. "You can learn business skills, typing and filing. And you're sure to make friends with some of the other women. It won't be too bad and then you'll be able to come back. And you'll feel better."

Then she added, "And don't worry, I forgive you for trying to seduce Thomas. Here, let me do your nails."

She reached for the polish that sat between them, but Maybelle pulled her hands away.

"Can't. This won't go with yellow." She pushed herself from the tiny chair and walked around the small area, making circles around Gladys.

Gladys rolled her eyes. She was trying to smooth things over. Despite all that Maybelle had done, she was still her twin, and she felt sorry for her. She tried to show affection by offering to do her nails, but even that simple gesture was turning into more work than she wanted to invest.

"Do you think anyone else ever comes down here?" Maybelle asked as she brushed past Gladys.

"No, never. Just you and me. And I haven't been down here in ages."

"Remember playing down here? Like it was our own house? We'd use that old garden rake and pretend it was a broom?"

Gladys smiled and laughed. "It was so heavy, neither of us could really lift it, but we'd still fight over who got to sweep."

"Ha! It's still here." Maybelle pulled the rake from where it leaned on the wall and drug it behind her. "It's still heavy," she mumbled.

"Be careful," Gladys said. "That old rusty thing is still sharp, too. The tines are making rows in the dirt!"

Maybelle stopped behind Gladys and sighed. "I can't believe you don't see this coming."

"What don't I-,"

The rake landed on Gladys's head, knocking her to the ground while puncturing the skin where it hit. Small rivers of blood trickled down her face.

She held her hand up, palm out, trying to ward off another blow.

"Stop," she moaned, but Maybelle didn't hesitate. She pulled the tines from Gladys's head and swung again. This time, she aimed for her neck. One tine struck just right. Maybelle watched impatiently as Gladys gurgled, trying to breathe and speak as blood pooled beneath her.

Maybelle was aware of the others in the room, but she steadfastly ignored them. She wanted to reenact the scene exactly as it had happened.

When it was over, she bent down and pulled the tiny diamond from her sister's finger and placed it on her own left hand. Then she rolled Gladys up in the small rug and dragged her to the back corner of the cellar. It was hard work, but she lifted the lifeless body onto the shelf. Then she shoved as hard as she could. No one ever came down here, and it was always so cold. She would come back down later and do the hard work of moving the body back as far as she could. There might be an odor, she knew, but if she could move her towards a vent, it might just work. She could hide her there with no problems.

She was sweating and exhausted, almost as much as she was the first time she did this for real all those decades ago.

Connie and Joe were blocking the stairs as though they could stop her. She pushed through them and then paused and turned back to say a few final words. It was the only time she broke character throughout the entire thing. She was proud of herself. It was a wonderful show.

She climbed back up the stairs, listening carefully for any sounds from her parents. She knew they weren't there, but she was determined to relive every single second exactly as it had been. It was her reward for all the hard work she'd put in over the years.

Maybelle darted up the stairs and into Gladys's room. She grabbed a pink nightgown and then ran to the bathroom. She didn't really need a bath but went through the motions anyway, pretending to wash away the blood and sweat and dirt. Standing in front of the mirror, she smiled to herself as she pulled the pink nightgown on and went into Gladys's bedroom.

She slept soundly that night, under a pink blanket.

～

Thomas was pretty spry for an old guy. He leapt forward to catch the falling body of Gladys after the first strike. She slipped through his fingers and fell to the ground. He dropped beside her and held his hand up in a futile attempt to stop Maybelle's second strike. It was pointless. The rake went right through him as though he were the ghost.

Maybelle continued with her mission as though none of them were there. She rolled the body in the rug and hefted and shoved it onto the dirt shelf. She climbed up after it, pushing and shoving it as far back as she could.

Joe and I watched as she scooted back out, wiping the dust from her body. She completely ignored Thomas and stood before the two of us.

"What you don't know is that they were going to send me away. They didn't want me here. They didn't love me, they only loved her. I had no choice. And now that I'm dead too, I refuse to spend eternity with her. I called you here to get rid of her."

She glanced behind her as the bottom of Thomas's feet could be seen scooting further under the house, in the direction she had just come from.

"This will happen every single night until she goes. And if you try anything, it just might happen to you too. Don't be a hero, Connie. Get rid of Gladys, and you and I will be just fine here. And for god's sake, get rid of the damn cat, too."

I can only imagine the look on my face. I knew my mouth was hanging open, goosebumps covered every inch of my body, and I was shaking. I'd faced other spirits before, other hostile and angry ones, other violent ones, but I'd never felt the venom that came from Maybelle. I'd never been personally threatened.

I was terrified.

Joe put an arm around me as Maybelle pushed her way past us and disappeared from view just before reaching to the top of the steps. As an ultimate insult, the door to the cellar slammed shut.

"We have to get moving," Joe said. "Get Thomas and let's get out of here."

In a trance, I called for Thomas. When he didn't reply, I panicked. He had to be eighty, maybe even older, and what he was doing had to be taking a lot out of him. Not to mention the emotional toll he'd just experienced watching his fiancé murdered in front of him.

I wasn't proud of myself, but all I could think about was what if another old person died in the house in the same week? I felt like that might cast a little suspicion on me. I was still waiting for the police to show up regarding Gladys and then, if Thomas died too, what would I say? How would I explain why we were in the basement?

I needn't have worried. Within a few more seconds, I heard huffing and grunting and saw the bottom of Thomas's shoes wiggling towards the edge. I went to him and guided his legs down over the dirt bench and the retaining wall until he stood. He had dragged what appeared to be a rolled-up rug behind him. When he reached the edge of the wall, he gently turned the rug sideways and handed me the flashlight.

Then he slowly unrolled the rug.

My heart stopped when I saw what I already knew was there. The sound of Thomas's wail tore through me. It represented decades of heartbreak and loneliness. Of not being able to mourn his love or even to move on. Of not knowing the truth, but suspecting the absolute worst. And having to live across the street from all that, facing it day after day. No wonder he was so bitter towards Gladys. Or the woman I thought was Gladys, but was actually Maybelle in disguise.

I felt a warm spot on my shoulder and turned to see Joe. He was pointing to the opposite corner where another apparition floated. I hoped to hell this was a nice one. If it wasn't, we were going to be in serious trouble.

The form glided towards Thomas and, much as Joe had touched my shoulder, she touched Thomas. From his reaction, it was obvious this was the real Gladys. Thomas stood and faced her, pure rapture on his face, his eyes shining in what light there was.

Then he fell to the ground, dead.

CHAPTER 12

"Oh, come on!" Samantha wasn't having any of it. "I don't believe this. So now you've got three ghosts in the house? Plus Joe? Connie, this is crazy."

I nodded as she fussed. She was right. It was pure insanity. And it was only getting worse. I had two warring factions in the house. Maybelle and Gladys for one and now, instead of going back to his own home, I also had Thomas slinking around in ghostly form. He refused to leave without Gladys, and she couldn't leave. And she still couldn't talk to us. Not to Thomas or Joe, and definitely not to me.

Maybelle just laughed and laughed. She let me know she was prepared to repeat the scenario of the murder repeatedly, leaving Thomas and Gladys in a kind of living hell. She terrorized Joe, too, appearing out of nowhere and slashing at him with knives. Of course, she couldn't hurt him, but it was disconcerting. She threatened to catch Brodie on fire, too. The final straw was her constant threats to me, that I'd end up like Gladys if I didn't do something quickly.

She wanted me to get rid of Gladys and Thomas, immediately.

"Then I can have the house again. It should be mine anyway," she nonchalantly commented one morning.

I didn't remind her she's a ghost and can't really own anything. I didn't want to give her ideas or garner her wrath again. We were all walking on eggshells, especially me, since I was the only one left to be killed.

"What are you going to do?" Samantha asked. "Are you coming back home?"

"I don't know that I can. I can't just leave things here the way they are. I've got to help them."

"Connie, is it really your problem? You didn't know any of these people two weeks ago and now you're in the middle of this incredible drama. Why is it your responsibility?"

"Because the house is mine," I replied lamely.

"That doesn't mean the ghosts within it are yours too," Samantha shot back.

"Still, there's more to it-," I tried to explain, but Sam cut me off before I could finish my sentence.

"There's always more to it." She said flatly.

She was right. But it didn't matter. The situation was what it was, and I had to be there. I didn't know why and I didn't know what I was supposed to do, but I knew I couldn't leave. At least not yet. I also knew I needed help, and as much as I dreaded it, I called Tawny.

She picked up before the phone even rang. "I'll be there in five hours. My flight is at 3:00 and I'm leaving for the airport right now."

I didn't even ask. She just knew and really, I was grateful. Still, this was going to be annoying.

True to her word, Tawny pulled up roughly five hours later. I'd spent the time talking to the police and having not just

Thomas's body removed, but also Gladys's. Forensics was all over the place and if it weren't for the fact that I wasn't even born when she died, I worried I might be in trouble.

When I explained to them that "Gladys" had died and then Thomas came over and went into the basement with me, then he died, they looked at me as though I'd grown a second head. It was a twisted and confusing story. Still, it was my story, and I was sticking to it.

I met Tawny on the porch just as the police were pulling away.

"How did that go?" She asked, throwing a look over her shoulder.

"About as expected."

I answered her and then pulled her into a tight hug. "Thank you. I know you just got home and then turned around to come back. Thank you so much."

"Don't sweat it. I figured I'd be back, anyway. Yeah, it was sooner than I expected, but it's all good."

I led her upstairs, where she settled her into the room she had recently vacated. I hadn't done a lick of laundry or cleaning either. She didn't care and started unpacking immediately. She'd brought enough clothes for a month.

"I'll leave you to it," I said, getting bored waiting for her. "Meet me downstairs when you're ready."

"Will do!"

She appeared thirty minutes later. I was in the sitting room, feet tucked under me, curled into my chair. I gestured towards a bottle of wine that sat on the coffee table and the extra glass I'd brought out.

Gladys had a robust wine cabinet stocked with a wide selection of local wines, as well as several unique vintages. I had grand plans for my virtual vineyard tour, but it would have to wait.

"Tell me what's been happening over the last twenty-four hours," Tawny began. "I know some of what's going on, but the feelings I picked up early this morning were strong enough to send me online to book a flight. I knew you needed some backup soon."

I smiled at my young, yet incredibly sensitive and intuitive, friend.

"You are absolutely correct. It's become a madhouse here. Gladys and Maybelle have fought even more violently. They are banging around, making a terrible racket. Now we have Thomas in the mix, too. While he's not part of the fighting, he's caught up in the drama and gets dragged into it every time. He's not a powerful spirit either, at least not yet. Then there's what Maybelle is doing to Joe. He's constantly threatened and accosted, and...,"

"What?"

"And she's threatened me, too. She says she's going to do to me what she did to Gladys."

"She's threatened to kill you? That's not possible. She can't! She's a ghost." Tawny's confident words made me feel better, but it didn't last.

"She can make it pretty miserable though," I added.

"And what is Joe's take on all of this?"

"I'll let you tell him yourself."

As if he had been listening, which he probably was, Joe appeared next to Brodie.

"Hey Joe," Tawny said calmly. It was nice to have someone around who could see him and not require a full explanation.

"Hey," he waved, then drifted to the sofa. He sat beside Tawny and turned to face her.

"I've told Connie all of this already. We've had a few back and forths on what the best solution is. I'm happy you're here."

Tawny nodded along as he talked. Their relationship

had started a little rocky, but after Joe saved us both from a malignant spirit in an old plantation house on the outskirts of Charleston, he had won her heart. She didn't even flinch at the idea of sitting next to Brodie the Beaver on the flight.

Strange child.

"I'm happy to be here too," she said. "I only hope I can help."

Joe sighed deeply and cut his eyes towards me. I swear every day I could see more detail on his face. I wondered if Tawny did, too. Was it Joe or was it me just accepting him?

He told her what happened that morning and the show Maybelle forced us all to witness.

She listened with eyes wide and mouth opening and closing as though she had something to say but couldn't find the words.

"That is the most heartbreaking love story I've ever heard." She actually swiped away a tear and then looked from Joe to me and then added, "Well, except for yours, of course."

Ours? Joe and I looked at each other. Did we have a love story? And it was heartbreaking? I laughed uncomfortably, vowing to ask Tawny what she meant later.

For now, I found it interesting that she was more concerned about the love story than about the actual murder that was being reenacted in my cellar. I started to ask her why, but stopped when my phone rang.

It was Peyton, and the spirit in my house was raising hell. Literally and figuratively.

～

I could hear Hannah in the background.

"Morty! Morty come here now!" She called her dog in a frantic voice.

And then the sound of a rumble that made me think of thunder or a train. But they were in the house.

"Peyton! What is happening?"

"It's your ghost mom. It's angry about something. It hasn't been like this before."

"Put her on speaker," Tawny said and moved closer to the phone. Joe did the same.

"You're on speaker," I shouted. The bangs and crashes were coming through loud and clear, but the voices of my children were fading.

"Peyton, you both need to get out of the house right now!" Tawny yelled through the phone.

We listened to the sounds of scuffles and snuffles, which I assume were Morty, Hannah's pit bull, the gentlest and sweetest creature ever. Then I heard the creak of the door opening. Finally, it was quiet.

"Okay, we're sitting on the front steps. It sounds like the noises have stopped." Peyton reported in between breaths.

"Are you both okay? Morty?" I asked.

"Yeah, we're all fine. Just a little shaken," Hannah chimed in. "Morty's good. He's sitting on me."

"What the hell is going on down there?" I asked.

"Well, get comfortable," Hannah said.

"Yeah, it's a long story," Peyton added.

"How long can it be? We just talked last night!"

CHAPTER 13

*P*eyton explained how she'd come to the house shortly after I left. She was prepared with a spirit box, an EVP, and an open mind. She was determined to get to the bottom of whatever was happening in the house.

Having seen ghosts and spirits since childhood, Peyton was comfortable with the unknown. She lied when I asked her about the ghosts she saw as a child. Hannah admitted she did, too. Neither one wanted me to worry.

Peyton also didn't mention that since the moratorium had ended, her own abilities had grown in leaps and bounds. Again, she didn't want to worry me or derail me from my own experiences.

"You're the best, mom. But you do tend to drop everything and rush to us whenever something isn't exactly perfect for us," Hannah said.

"It's like a martyr thing. You always put us, or dad, really, anyone else ahead of your own needs," Peyton added.

"It was nice when we were young. Like we always knew you had our backs. But now-."

"Yeah, now, we kind of don't need that anymore. We'd love to see you doing your own thing," Peyton finished.

"Okay, okay. I hear you. Move on with your story. What's going on?"

Peyton was in a good mood. She remembered when Joe was first showing up. One of the very first signs of his presence was when we were going to throw away the taxidermy beaver and he kept moving it.

"Yeah, good times," I said.

She laughed and continued to reflect on how much she loved the house. Not only because it's where she grew up, but also because she felt a connection to the ghosts she'd seen there as a child. She desperately needed to reconnect with them.

Here Hannah chimed in. "Me too. About the ghosts I mean. I don't really want to live here."

"Thank you for your input," Peyton said mockingly.

I heard the sound of Hannah blowing a raspberry, followed by the sound of a hand hitting skin.

"Ow! Stop it!"

"You stop!"

"Girls!" I yelled into the phone.

A moment of silence was followed by Peyton continuing her story. She found the homemade and frozen food, as well as the diet Cokes, and planned a quiet evening in front of the TV, taking advantage of the movie channels I still paid for.

She began to see movement out of the corner of her eye and knew she wasn't alone.

"Was it the ghost that attacked those guys?" I asked.

"I don't know. It didn't bother me. I wasn't scared at all. In fact, that's why I called you that day to make sure dad was with you. I kinda thought it might be him checking up on me. I knew you had Brodie, but I didn't know for sure that you also had dad."

After she confirmed Joe was with me, she set up a control center in the kitchen and began trying to communicate with whoever or whatever was living there.

She spoke to it multiple times and through various avenues, trying to make it as easy as she could for it to communicate back. But nothing happened.

The next day, she called Hannah to come over.

"Of course she brought Morty with her," Peyton added.

I had no doubt. Morty went everywhere with Hannah. He was incredibly high maintenance, but when you saw him with her, it was the most precious thing. Morty and Hannah were a team.

Peyton continued. From what she said, they had a good old-fashioned sleep over. They watched movies, ate popcorn, and made margaritas.

Apparently, that's when things took a turn. Whatever was there did not like their raucous fun or their loudness.

It started banging pots and pans and throwing dishes and flatware at them. Poor Morty was hit with a flying spatula at one point.

They cleaned up each time, but as soon as they thought everything calmed down, drawers would open and cutlery would be dumped on the floor. Trash cans were overturned. The refrigerator was left open.

"It was like a poltergeist went through here. But I told it I wasn't scared. Instead, I knew it was unhappy, and I wanted to help."

"How did that go?" Tawny asked cautiously.

"It completely ignored me and kept tearing up the house. That was the first time you called and Hannah answered."

I knew something was up. Hannah was always the better liar, and Peyton would never let her phone die.

She finished by telling us they were tired of cleaning up after this thing and was there any way I could get it to stop acting up.

They weren't calling because they were scared. They were calling because they were tired of picking up after it.

～

～

"Why did you let it get this bad before calling me?" I asked. These kids were exasperating.

"It really only got super bad this morning," Peyton said. "Before this, we've been handling it."

"Now it seems like it's really mad, though. And we don't know why." Hannah added. "Can you do something?"

I looked at Tawny for advice.

She was hunched over. Elbows on her knees, chin resting in both hands, staring intently at the cellphone. Either she was deep in thought or she'd fallen asleep.

Of course, it was the former. She finally spoke.

"Peyton, Hannah, I don't think you are in danger. I believe it is a daemon in the house, but... no, wait, hear me out."

She was interrupted by four voices, asking at once how a demon could not be dangerous. This wasn't an area I had any experience with, nor Peyton or Hannah. Joe looked as though he were trying to teleport through the phone. That fatherly protective instinct had gone nowhere.

Tawny held up her hands and waved them at the two of us who could see her. Out loud she said, "Listen. I know that sounds strange, but it really isn't all that unusual. Daemons aren't evil. You're thinking of demons. Different spelling, different entities. Daemons are kind of like guardian angels. They've been around forever and while they technically aren't good or evil, they are honorable and intelligent. Some can even control a person, to a degree."

"Are you thinking that this daemon, or whatever, is there to protect us?" Peyton asked. "Because I'll tell you, when things are flying around the room, knives and stuff, it sure doesn't feel like it wants to protect anything."

"Sure, I understand that. But remember how it protected Connie?" Tawny looked up at me and smiled. "At the time, we all thought it was Joe. Or you all did anyway. I wasn't really convinced, but I didn't have another option to offer." Tawny looked at Joe and added, "Not that you wouldn't have wanted to protect her. But at the time, I couldn't believe you could manifest like that. Not yet. You know, it takes time to learn."

Joe nodded along as she spoke, trying not to offend the ghost of my deceased. He smiled and flapped his hand at her. "You can stop. I know what you're saying. Either way, my feelings right now aren't the issue. Safety in Charleston is."

When he said the part about his feelings not being the issue, he sent me a rather pointed look, as if to say he knew I'd agree to that assessment. Yet another thing to worry about. His feelings were still hurt.

"Anyway," Tawny continued, "it's not there to harm. I really believe that. How many years have you lived there, and it's never hurt anyone until Connie was specifically targeted? And she's been gone now for over a week and other people are living there. It hasn't hurt either of you and we know it could if it wanted to. No, guys, I think it's confused and maybe worried. And it's acting out the only way it knows how."

"I've tried to talk to it. Like really tried. All the gadgets and opportunities, different times, different ways. It's not talking to me. That's why I, we, called."

Tawny grew quiet for a few moments.

"Hello?" Hannah said.

"We're here. Tawny is thinking. I don't know what to say. I don't have anything to add," I said.

Finally Tawny lifted her head again and spoke.

"Orenda will come to you tonight. She believes she has some insight into this situation and might be able to help."

"What? Were you just-. Did you just talk to her? Right now?" I was stunned. The amazing shit never stopped around here.

Tawny smiled sheepishly. "Yeah, it's a thing," she said. Then she grew serious and professional. "Remember how I told you it's all connected?" I nodded as Peyton's voice come over the line.

"What's connected? Who are you talking to?"

"All of you," Tawny said. "It is all connected. My mother has known about your family forever. She's known about the moratorium and all that you've experienced. In fact, so does Madame from the conference."

"Ah yes, the network of ghostly spies that have been watching us for decades. Lovely and not at all creepy."

I remember when she told me this. It made me profoundly uncomfortable, and I pushed it from my mind. I didn't want to think about it. All I could picture was me doing something embarrassing and having it reported throughout the spirit realm to everyone else. Like a gossip chain in the ether.

"It's not like that. It's more like a community. And the spirit world, those entities, is how the community communicates. No one is making fun of you or laughing at you for doing something embarrassing."

"You're reading my mind again," I muttered.

"It's not that hard, Connie," she paused. "Listen, you've trusted me for the past year when things have gotten serious. Joe trusts me. And Orenda has taught you so much, you obviously trust her too. I'm asking you to continue to trust us through this part, too. We don't have all the answers, but I think we are better positioned to find them."

"It's different now. This involves my kids and their safety. This changes everything."

~

Despite my objections, which no one seemed to care about, Orenda was dispatched to my old house in Charleston.

I really wanted the girls to go back to their homes and stop messing with this altogether. It simply wasn't safe, and we were tinkering with things we didn't understand.

Tawny continued to argue that just because we didn't understand, it doesn't mean she and Orenda didn't.

"You just have to trust us. You can trust Orenda, can't you?"

I was grateful to have Orenda involved. She was also a mother and would recognize my worries. She even called me to help put my mind at ease.

"It is okay," she said in her deep southern drawl that somehow also sounded mystical. "I won't let any harm come to your children. Or your house. Just let me in there for a while. I have an inkling to what's going on. I'll get to the bottom of it."

I thanked Orenda and asked if she would keep the kids out of the house while she was working. She stuttered and sputtered a little and then answered rather cryptically. "I won't ask them to come in."

Then she hung up.

Won't ask them? While she wouldn't actually say anything to them, I could easily picture her standing on my porch, holding the door open for them. Of course, not saying a word because she said she promised she wouldn't "ask" them.

Fine. I gave up. They were adults. Orenda knew what she was doing. I was almost a thousand miles away. Fine.

"You're pouting," Joe said.

Tawny had retired to her room. The mental connection she had with Orenda had tired her out and she wanted to close her eyes and rest. That left Joe and me in the sitting room. It was very quiet, which wasn't good. It left me alone with my thoughts, and he was right. I was pouting.

"Yeah, well. I have reason to."

"I understand. I'm worried too. But we have to trust that we did all we could. That they will make the right choices for themselves. They have so far, haven't they?"

I nodded. Yes, they were both pretty amazing. They had carved a life for themselves and they were happy. Although neither one's life looked a thing like what I would have chosen for them, it was easy to throw support behind them. They really were pretty amazing.

"What was with that look you shot me?" I asked, changing the subject. This seemed like as good a distraction as anything.

"What look?"

"When you were talking about how this isn't about you and your feelings, you gave me a dirty look."

"Yeah, I guess I did. But you haven't considered my feelings in a long time. And I know, I know, you don't have to say anything. I know I didn't act like I considered yours for how many years before. I know, I get it. Payback's a bitch."

Payback? Did he think I was getting some sort of revenge?

138

"Joe, I'm not trying to pay you back for anything. I haven't deliberately tried to make you feel bad. It's not that at all."

I said the words, but in the back of my mind, I wasn't so sure they were accurate. Maybe I was unconsciously getting revenge. He was right, after all. I didn't consider his feelings. I complained all the time about lugging Brodie around, but I wasn't the one attached to a stuffed beaver compulsively telling everyone to hang loose. I teased him about sitting down and putting his feet up, but it never occurred to me he was doing those things to make me feel more comfortable. He was trying to do as much normally as he could. I sent him away whenever I wanted and I shut myself off from him unless I needed something. And I wasn't very nice.

Crap, he was right. And now I was crying.

When Joe died, things changed so quickly. I went from being a stay at home mom with no kids at home, to being some type of witch who was also an empath and intuitive. I could see and talk to ghosts, not just that of my husband, but others too. I started working in that very field just a few months later. I learned about my family and the moratorium. I learned about my own mother and a little about my grandmother. I had Tawny and her mother in my life and they opened up a whole new world to me. I was learning about so many things that were unique and new and I supposed I had lumped Joe in with all of that.

But he was different. He was my husband. And he was still with me. I was taking it for granted. When I allowed myself to think, for just a moment, what it would be like to be sitting here by myself right this minute. To not have him in the same room, regardless of the form he took, the single tear turned into a flood. I sobbed, my body shaking. I felt guilty and angry with myself. Sad and overwhelmed. Afraid and worried.

Joe moved next to me. I could feel the shift in the air around me as he swirled into being. He put his arm around my shoulders and I felt the familiar warmth spread throughout my back and arms. I closed my eyes and rested in his embrace. I felt myself pulled towards him and my head rested on his chest. It was lovely. I felt calm for the first time in ages. I tucked my feet under me and stretched into his arms.

Wait! How was I doing that? How was I not sinking through him and laying on the sofa, my face where his ghostly crotch would be?

"Joe?" I whispered.

"Yes?"

I opened one eye and looked at what was in my limited vision. It was Joe. His body was supporting mine. I wasn't sinking through. I could actually feel him.

"What's happening?"

"You're finally seeing me. Remember Connie? I told you it all comes from you, not me. You're making this happen."

I was making this happen. I had control over this. It was amazing and frightening. But mostly, it felt fantastic to feel his body next to mine. To feel the warmth of his chest. It flickered through my mind that I shouldn't be able to feel a ghost like this. But I pushed the questions aside and simply enjoyed the moment. There would be plenty of time for questions and answers later. Now, for the first time in ages, I could rest.

CHAPTER 14

"*T*hat must be her."

Orenda flung the door open and stepped from the backseat of the car. She reached in and pulled a bag from the other side and then turned.

Peyton and Hannah watched the tiny woman in the long skirt. She had long, grey hair pulled into a ponytail. An interesting choice for someone her age. Her top was sleeveless and gauzy, flowing along with her skirt. She seemed to be barefoot.

Peyton and Hannah had heard about Orenda from their own mother and from Tawny. They knew a little about her past and her story. They also knew she was the best shot they had of getting back into the house soon, without having cutlery flying towards them.

They stood and waited while she picked her way along the walk.

"Hello," she said when she was close enough to be heard.

"Here, can I help?" Hannah reached out and took the bag from Orenda. It looked heavy, especially for her slight frame.

"Thank you, darling," she huffed.

"I'm Peyton, and this is Hannah. Oh, and this is Morty. Are you okay with dogs?"

Orenda smiled. "Oh, my yes. I love dogs. Any animal, really."

Normally, Morty would jump up and down, trying his best to get to the new person in his life. He was friendly and sweet, but he loved people a little too much. He believed everyone wanted to be his best friend just as much as he wanted to be theirs.

Now, though, he was sitting quietly on the porch, just beyond Hannah's reach. He waited patiently for Orenda.

"Be careful," Hannah warned. "He's very friendly. He might jump."

Orenda laughed and reached out. Morty scooted underneath her outstretched hand and allowed her to rub his head and ears.

"Who's a sweet boy? Huh? He's a good boy, inn't he?"

Hannah looked at Peyton, who shrugged. So much for the mystical intimidation.

Finally, Orenda stood and cracked her back. "Well, ladies, shall we?"

They nodded. Peyton opened the door. Orenda went first, true to her word, not saying anything. She needn't have worried. Peyton and Hannah followed on her heels. Morty, however, hesitated. Orenda flicked a finger in his direction and he followed her in. He sat beside her, watching her every move, alert to further command.

"What have you done to my dog?" Hannah asked. "I've never seen him so calm before."

Orenda simply smiled and ignored the question. It was rhetorical anyway.

She paused in the foyer and looked around the spacious area. It was a wonderful open floor plan and she could see the kitchen, dinette and sitting room from where she stood. To her right was an odd room. It looked as though a large closet had been plunked down in the middle of the room and shoved to the side.

"That's Dad's office," Hannah offered. "His man cave. It's where he stays when he's here." Then she seemed to rethink what she said. "You do know about our dad, right?"

Orenda nodded. "Yes, I know all about your father, your mother, and your family. I have a connection with the spirit world that allows me to find out most anything I need. It might take time, but I can put out a request and find out what I need to know within a week or less."

Peyton nodded. "Sort of like internet but with ghosts?"

Hannah joined in, laughing. "Ghost Google!"

They both laughed, proud of their joke, but Orenda simply stood watching them. It didn't help that Morty had the same disinterested look on his face, too. Peyton and Hannah sobered quickly.

Peyton cleared her throat. "Where would you like to start?"

Orenda walked purposely into the sitting room, directly to a chair under the front window, and sat. She closed her eyes and laid her head back. Morty irritatingly sat beside her as though protecting her.

Hannah gestured for him to come to her. He looked at her, but then turned his head away from the only person in his life who fed and loved him. The one who always played with him and let him sleep in her bed. Prior to meeting Orenda, he never ever allowed himself to be separated from Hannah, much less chosen to do so.

Hannah whisper yelled, "Morty. Come here, come! Morty! Now. Come!" He continued to ignore her and Hannah gave up. She and Peyton stood in the foyer, still holding Orenda's bag. They looked at each other and then at Orenda.

"Is she asleep?" Hannah whispered.

Peyton shrugged. "Put the bag down and let's go into the kitchen. Maybe she needs quiet or whatever."

They made their way through the dinette and settled in the kitchen. They could still see Orenda through the pass-through, but were far enough away that their lowered voices were unlikely to bother her.

While Connie and Joe were a thousand miles away rekindling their relationship, Peyton and Hannah were wondering if their mother would return to Charleston.

They both said, "Not."

"What do you think she'll do with the house?"

"I don't know. Do you want it?" Peyton asked. "You're getting married. Probably have a family soon. It would be a nice place."

Hannah agreed. "But I don't think so. Lewis and I already have a place. And we like it there. I don't want to move. What about you? You could live here. Move out of the apartment, have more space. You love this house so much."

"What would I do with all this space?" Peyton asked.

Hannah laughed. "Now you sound like Mom. You would just have the space. What's the problem?"

"One of you will have to live here."

Orenda's voice made them both jump. Hannah let out a slight squeal and held her hand over her heart.

"Good grief! You scared me!" She said.

At the same time Peyton exclaimed, "Dammit!" And turned to face her.

"One of you will have to live here. Either of you," Orenda wagged her finger between Peyton and Hannah, "Or your mother will need to come back. Or, there's a grandmother too. Right? She could make it work."

Orenda ignored the startled reactions and went on.

"Otherwise, I fear no one will be able to live here. It would take an awful lot to get him to leave."

She muttered to herself and passed through the room into the hallway. The girls followed her. She paused with one foot on the stairs and her hand resting on the railing.

"What do you mean?" Peyton asked.

Orenda didn't answer and began climbing the stairs slowly. With each step, she paused and tested the board under her foot as though she feared she would fall through.

Once again, Peyton and Hannah looked at each other and shrugged. This was a strange woman. They had no idea what she was doing, but could only hope there would be a solution to the problem. Since she had been in the house, it was completely quiet. No banging or thumping. Nothing flying from cabinets and no cutlery shooting through the air.

Unfortunately, the same couldn't be said for where Connie was.

I woke up when I heard the loud crash. I'd been asleep in Joe's arms for the first time in ages. It had been pure bliss, but now it was over. As though there wasn't enough going on in Charleston, now something was going on here. Again.

Tawny rushed from her room, wild-eyed, hair sticking out at all angles, makeup smudged.

"What the hell?" She asked.

"That's why I called you," I told her. "That's what we've been dealing with."

"It's Maybelle and Gladys. They are fighting."

"What about Thomas?" Tawny asked.

"He seems like he wants to help, but Maybelle hates him

so much. He's sort of staying out of the way." Joe explained as much as he could glean.

"Gladys still doesn't talk either." I said. "Remember, they are switched now. The woman we thought was Gladys was actually Maybelle. And Maybelle is who killed the actual Gladys."

"Uh huh, right. And then Maybelle pretended to be Gladys for all these years. And only Thomas suspected it, right?"

Joe and I nodded.

"Well, I think the first thing we need to do is get Thomas out of the way. Then we can figure out what to do. They both can't stay here. Maybelle has to leave. Did you ever find out why she left the house to you?"

"No, no idea at all."

"I'm really curious about why she did that." Tawny said. "It's out of character for what we know about her. There must be some reason."

"She won't tell me. Maybe you can you get some answers?"

Tawny began wandering through the bed-and-breakfast, listening carefully, holding her hands in front of her. She worked silently. Taking a small step and then listening intently. She appeared as though in a trance. Her eyes were unfocused and glazed over, yet she knew exactly where she was going.

When she wandered away from us, I whispered to Joe.

"I guess she's finding out something. Maybe she can communicate with Gladys now."

"Yeah, maybe." He didn't sound very convincing.

"I want to call the kids," I said.

Joe nodded, and we huddled in a corner of the room. I held the phone between us and hit send.

Peyton answered immediately.

"How's it going there?" I asked in a hushed voice. I felt compelled to make myself small and as quiet as possible.

"Hannah and I are standing in a corner of the sitting room," Peyton whispered. "Orenda is walking around like a zombie. Looking everywhere and stopping a lot. Like she's listening. Why? What's going on there?"

"Well, pretty much the same thing. Except it's Tawny who's the zombie."

"What are they doing, Mom?" Hannah asked. Also in a hushed whisper.

"I don't know," I confessed. "I thought Tawny was dealing with my ghosts, but now I wonder."

"So we just keep huddling in the corner? Afraid to move or even talk too loud?" Peyton asked.

"Hey, kids," Joe said. "Can you hear me?"

"Dad? Wow! You're doing great! Yes, we can hear you."

"Just try to stay calm, okay. I don't know what's happening either, but I know this is going to work out."

"Yeah, okay," Hannah said.

I could hear her whisper to Peyton. "I can't believe how well we can hear him."

Peyton's reply was muffled, but I gathered she was agreeing with her sister.

"Wait," Peyton then said. "Orenda is back. She's just standing there with her eyes closed."

At the same time, Tawny also reappeared in the sitting room. She too stood stock still in the middle of the room, eyes closed.

"Weird...," Peyton exhaled the single word.

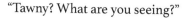

"Tawny? What are you seeing?"

"It's a daemon for certain. Not a ghost. What are you seeing?"

"The same. Do you see the connection?"

"No, not yet. Do you?"

"Yes, I see it. I see it clearly."

"Can you show me?"

"No. You will have to see it for yourself to fully understand. It's okay, child. You're ready. Let it happen."

Tawny collapsed in the middle of the sitting room. Connie and Joe rushed to her side. Connie pulled her sitting and gently tapped her cheek.

"Tawny, are you okay?"

She nodded slowly and then she spoke in a strange, high-pitched, singsong voice.

"Move me to the sofa and then leave me alone. I have work to do."

Connie did as instructed and settled Tawny on the sofa. On her way out of the room, she turned back and tucked a throw blanket over her legs. Then she fluffed an extra pillow and tucked it behind her. The mothering instinct made her feel like she was doing something helpful. She was worried.

"What's happening now?" I asked when Joe and I left Tawny to her own devices in the other room.

"Orenda woke up. I guess that's how you'd put it, and then said she wanted to be alone. She sent us downstairs, and she went up to your room. She said something about watching Tawny but not being involved and that it took a lot of concentration."

"What does that mean?" Hannah asked when Peyton finished talking.

"I don't know, but Tawny is doing the same thing. She's on the sofa and wanted to be alone."

"Okay, well. I guess we'll just hang out down here," Peyton said. "Watch TV or something?" She said the last part as a question. I didn't blame her. I didn't know what to do either.

"Okay, we'll talk later?" I also said with my voice lilting up at the end.

"Okay. Bye."

"Bye."

I turned back to Joe. "Now what?"

"We wait."

CHAPTER 15

*T*awny looked around. She was back in time, maybe in the early 1800s, but she wasn't sure. There were no cars. Instead, horse-drawn buggies and wagons moved slowly down the street.

She saw an old woman, bent and crooked, standing in front of what appeared to be a grocery store. Although she knew that's not what they were called back then. She thought back to reruns of "Little House on the Prairie." Mercantile! That's what it was. She watched the old woman for a few moments, fearing she would tip over. She seemed very unsteady.

Tawny was certain she wouldn't be able to help her if something happened. She knew she couldn't be seen. It was obvious by the number of people who passed her and passed through her. Not animals, though. They knew.

It surprised her when the old woman looked directly into her eyes. Tawny stayed still, not moving a muscle, while she watched to see what the old woman would do.

She rubbed her eyes hard and shook her head sharply. She continued to stare at Tawny.

The intense scrutiny was getting to her, and out of instinct, Tawny lifted her hand and waved.

The woman waved back. And then she looked behind her, then up and down the street. Tawny wanted to tell her no one saw her wave. She didn't get the chance, though. The old woman turned and hurried away in the opposite direction.

Tawny felt like she should follow. She didn't know what else to do, but the old woman disappeared quickly and she lost track of her directions. There was a commotion down the road and she turned towards it.

A group of men gathered in front of the saloon. They were arguing about another man. No, it was a boy. Tawny listened as closely as she dared. She wasn't sure who else could see her, and she knew enough to know she didn't want to draw their attention to her.

Eventually she heard that a boy, a teenager, named William was harming the young women in the small town. They suspected he had kidnapped a girl and had her in the basement of his house. They set out to make things right.

Tawny heard this story before. If she was correct and her memory served, she was watching the very reason they placed the moratorium on Connie's family. The girl trapped in the cellar was, unfortunately, dead, and it was just a matter of time before the mob made its way to the house. There they would hang the boy from a tree in the front yard and a witch, a relative of Connie's, would curse the house and the spirits of all who lived there.

The problem was, there was a little girl in the house. When the mob approached, William hid his sister, Ruthie, in a closet. He pushed a bureau in front of the door, trying to keep her safe. With their parents away at the World's Fair, he was in charge of her safety. Despite his evil heart, he wanted to protect her.

Tawny stood on the edges of the crowd, fairly certain she couldn't be seen, but still nervous. She also wanted to be close enough to witness all the events.

As she watched, all the stories she'd heard were confirmed, one after the other. The mob rushed into the house and into the cellar. A woman followed them in. Everyone outside could hear a piercing wail when she saw the body of her daughter.

The mob pulled the boy from the house. He struggled and fought, but it was useless. There were too many men, and they easily overpowered him. Tawny could hear him pleading for someone to save his sister, but the men ignored him and wrestled a rope around his neck.

As they prepared to hang the boy, the poor mother came from the house. She was supported on both sides by women, who gently guided her to the back of the crowd.

Soon the boy swayed from the tree, and the crowd cheered. Tawny saw a flash of green light from the opposite side of the field.

She knew the curse had been cast and now not just William, but also Ruthie, were trapped in the house for eternity.

The repercussions were far-reaching. Decades of abuse, terror and secrets haunted all those who lived in that house from then on. Only when two generations of women who grew up in the house banded together were they finally able to defeat the evil that had ruled their family.

Tawny thought about all she knew, and while she was understanding more about the story of Ruthie, she was still confused. Why was she seeing all of this, and what did it have to do with the daemon in Charleston? And she felt bad that she was there for Connie and Joe, yet here she was, doing something that had nothing to do with the bed-and-breakfast.

She had no choice, though, so she continued to watch. Eventually, the mob left the yard and William's body swayed in the slight breeze. The choking and gasping sounds coming from his restricted windpipe stopped and his feet and hands stopped twitching.

She watched his spirit separate from his body and float towards the house. Shortly after that, the old woman from the mercantile appeared next to the tree. She looked up at the body and then looked at the house. She scratched her head, then turned towards Tawny.

She crooked her finger and beckoned Tawny closer.

Tawny looked behind her, thinking she was gesturing for someone else, but no one was there.

"Who? Me?" she asked, feeling foolish as she walked towards the woman.

"What are you?" She asked when Tawny was closer.

"I'm Tawny. I'm just watching."

"Tawny just watching," the old woman repeated.

"Why are you here Tawny just watching?"

"Um, no, it's just Tawny. You can drop the just watching part. And I don't know why I'm here. I'm trying to find out why a daemon is living in a friend's house."

"Just Tawny, where is this friend's house?"

Tawny sighed. Fine, her name was now Just Tawny. That wasn't the critical part of this.

"My friend is in the future. What year is this?"

"1893."

"Oh. Wow. Okay. Well, I'm from a long time from now. I'm trying to find out what happened here. I think there are answers here to some of our questions there."

The sound of twigs cracking behind them made both women turn. The old woman grabbed for Tawny's arm, but it went right through her.

"I'm not really here," she whispered.

"Follow me," the old woman said.

They moved steadily away from the body, positioning themselves in the darkness of the trees that surrounded the property. It was an eerie sight. The full moon hung low and the outline of the tree and William's body was clear. It was quiet. All the people from the mob had moved away from the house and gone to their own homes, quick to forget about what they had done.

A small group made their way to the tree. There were three of them. From this distance, they looked small and frail. Tawny assumed they were women. Old women.

"Friends of yours?" She whispered to the old woman by her side.

"Yes." She replied.

They watched as the women created a circle. They began to chant. Light danced between them and throughout their hands and fingers as they moved. Suddenly, a plume of black smoke shot up from the middle of their circle.

"Beezel," the old woman whispered.

The black smoke twisted and twirled in the air. The women stopped chanting and stood still.

Tawny could barely hear what was going on, but she thought she caught a few random words on the night air.

"Protect them, no matter what."

"They will need you when they can't do it themselves."

"Watch and wait."

Then the form evaporated into the night. The women rubbed their palms together and turned away from the circle. They walked away in opposite directions. Tawny turned to the old woman who was standing beside her. She was gone too.

"Wait!" she said.

Then she opened her eyes and looked around the sitting

room. She was covered by a cozy blanket, supported by a pile of pillows, and she was starving.

~

"Hey! Where is everyone?"

"Did you hear that?" I asked Joe.

He nodded as we headed back into the sitting room. I was relieved to see Tawny standing up, folding the blanket, and smiling.

"You're okay. Thank goodness," I gushed.

Tawny smiled. "I think I have some information. I can't make complete sense of it all yet, but I have a good start. I'll need to talk to Orenda."

We arranged that easily with a call to Orenda, who, according to Peyton, was still hanging around the house.

I called Peyton and told her a quick rundown of what was happening, and she immediately took the phone to Orenda.

"Is it her?"

I heard her ask in the background.

"Yeah, it's my mom," Peyton answered.

"No, I need Tawny," she said. "Put her on."

The command didn't sit well with me, but before Peyton put the phone in her hand, Tawny was standing beside me, taking the phone from mine.

"Mama," she said breathlessly into the phone. "Did you see it all?"

"Yes, I saw it."

I could barely hear Orenda through the phone and was hovering close by. After all, that was my house they were talking about, and my children, and apparently, my daemon.

"It's Beezel. I saw him and I heard his name."

Tawny looked over her shoulder at me. She put the

phone on speaker and held it in front of her. Joe was hovering nearby too, so it made it easier.

Orenda sighed at the name Beezel.

"That explains a lot. He's not the brightest one. It's okay though. At least we know what we're dealing with. Tell Connie, and Joe, that a daemon has been protecting them and theirs for decades, centuries really. I just need to let him know Peyton and Hannah are also yours. Then he'll back down and settle."

Tawny agreed and hung up. She looked at us with a smile that said we should be happy with the outcome.

As Tawny shared what she'd witnessed, it suddenly became very clear to me what she'd seen. She watched my own ancestors perform the very acts that created the need for the moratorium and had gotten us into trouble all these years. Then she watched as they summoned a daemon to protect us while our own powers were useless.

"Did they know Ruthie was in there?" I asked. "Why would they think we'd lose our powers otherwise? They had to have known they were doing something that would have consequences."

"Connie, I don't know. I hope not, but I just don't know."

She explained all that she saw.

"It's only purpose in its life is to protect your line. Your mother, you and the girls."

"And now, apparently, he's confused. How is it he recognized me but not the kids? And how come he didn't have a problem with them when they were younger?"

Tawny shook her head. "I don't know. You'll have to ask him."

"No, that's not going to work," I said. "I need answers.

156

He's down there, wreaking havoc on my house and putting my children in danger. And apparently it's something like a demon? What in the world? Is he dangerous?"

"No, remember? And he's a daemon, not a demon. There's a big difference. Our friend has powers and can get cranky, but basically, he's a good guy."

I calmed down a little, and then something else occurred to me.

"What about this house? What am I supposed to do with the warring sisters? And why am I even here? How did this happen?" I asked with my arms spread out, gesturing to the room in which we sat.

"I might be able to help with that."

We all froze. I looked at Joe and then Tawny. She looked at me and then at Joe. Joe looked at me, then Tawny. Then we looked at the cat.

Lex was sitting on the back of the sofa. He'd been there through all the conversations of the morning, calmly lying around, alternately scratching the furniture, purring, then dozing.

"Did you just talk?" I asked cautiously.

"Yes." Lex said. His voice was deep and husky, befitting the body he had. He sat with his tail wrapped around himself and his head held high. His green eyes glittered in the grey fur. I swear he was smiling.

"Okay then. I'm out."

～

I ignored the knocks on the bedroom door for as long as I could.

Tawny immediately followed me and wanted to discuss Lex. I told her to go away. Then Joe tried. I could hear Tawny hauling the beaver down the hallway so Joe could be close.

He was having trouble being very far away from it lately. Something that worried me a bit, but there were so many other things going on right now, I put that one lower on the list to be dealt with later.

I also ignored Joe as long as I could, then told him to go away too.

My mind was spinning. You would think after the year I just had that I wouldn't even flinch at a talking cat. I'd lost my husband, who came back as a ghost whom I could talk to and now see just as plainly as I could see anyone. Then I started working as a matchmaker for those who wanted a haunted house. And in that capacity, I interacted with ghosts and spirits on at least a weekly basis, sometimes more often than that.

I discovered these abilities coincided with the lifting of a moratorium that was placed on my family because I came from a line of witches who cursed a poor little girl. Now we could practice witchcraft, and those of us with intuitive skills and empaths could use our gifts fully. Tawny and her mother, Orenda, were in my life now, which was a good thing because they were teaching me things I needed to know. My own mother was still having a hard time with everything and ignored what was going on.

Added to that, I went to a conference where everyone had the same set of skills in some form or fashion and we all sat around asking a panel of ghosts questions. And let's not forget I was sitting in a bed-and-breakfast that was left to me by someone I didn't know but who was now haunting the house and threatening to murder us all, just as she had murdered her sister.

But apparently the one thing that broke me, the one thing that put me over the edge, was a talking cat. My mind refused to process it.

I just wanted a little bit of time alone to myself. I truly

wasn't sure I was going to find a place in my mind where this new information could live. And I was angry with myself for letting the one thing that might actually answer questions and be a support for me completely derail my thoughts and feelings.

I could hear scuffling noises outside my door. I froze, waiting to see which one of them was going to pester me again.

I was surprised to hear a deep and slightly husky voice.

"Connie. I know you're upset. Can I explain? I really think it will help."

"Let him talk Connie. He told Joe and me everything. It makes sense. It'll help."

So now the talking cat was outside my door. With Tawny. And they were trying to convince me to let him talk.

"Fine. Talk." I grumbled as I leaned on the closed door.

"Okay, well, Lex here isn't actually a cat," Tawny began.

"No, shit," I mumbled.

"I heard that. Anyway, he's also a daemon, well a type of daemon. He knows Beezel from your house."

"Uh huh," I nodded along at the insanity.

"Anyway, when you were making reservations for this trip, do you remember anything unique or strange? Like what led you to book this place in particular? There are a zillion other places, closer to the conference, maybe more comfortable." Her words trailed off. "But you chose this one. Why?"

I thought back to a month ago. I had no genuine memory of choosing this place. I found out we were going to the conference and Lisabeth asked me to find a place for us to stay. It fell into my duties as receptionist and office manager and it wasn't a problem. I surfed the web and had a few travel websites pulled up, thinking I would bundle the hotel and flight to save some money.

But every time I went back to the computer, this bed-and-breakfast was pulled up. I thought little it. I figured it was being advertised or was a special or something along those lines, so it would override whatever else was on the screen.

I reserved the flights, but was still looking at places to stay. Then one evening, I was scrolling through places. I left the computer open and got up for a drink. When I came back, this place was pulled up again. The dates were already populated and our contact information entered. Again, I thought very little about it, and I hit submit.

I told Tawny most of this as I stood on the other side of the door, leaning against it. I knew Lex was out there. His tail occasionally flicked under the door and I'd see a flash of grey. Part of me wanted to grab it. If he were a normal cat, I probably would have.

He finally spoke. "When Beezel found out you were leaving and where you were going, he contacted me. He knew I was here. So he made sure you would be here, with me, where I could keep an eye on you. Beezel is who pulled up this place and made sure it's where you ended up."

"Okay, but why did Gladys, or Maybelle or whoever, leave the place to me?"

"I made the old biddy do it," Lex said softly. "We knew she was going to die soon. All estimates from the reaper said it would likely be when you were here. If she didn't leave it to you, you would have gone back home and then I would have been left here, probably taken to a shelter." His voice cracked.

"This guaranteed I would be cared for. And it helped solve Beezel's problem of trying to keep you protected. Now that he knows about Peyton and Hannah being in the line, he will want to stay there for them. And I'll be here for you. It wasn't too difficult. She thought she was calling all the

160

shots and bringing you here to remove Gladys. She wanted to keep you around, believing she could control you, even after her death. But I was the one in control."

I'm not sure his explanation helped as much as he thought it would. Now I was stuck on the idea that they had some sort of communication set up between the two of them. And a daemon cat thing could control people? Would he try to control me? And make me do what exactly? Tawny read my mind, again.

"I know what you're thinking," she began. "You know, I've always told you we knew what was going to happen to you. We knew about the moratorium and we were watching. It's the same thing with them, except it was to protect you and your family. You simply haven't fully accepted it all and therefore haven't tapped into the community. There is much you have left to learn."

"Yeah, right. Okay, I'm opening the door now and coming out. Lex, do me a favor? Let's talk more later. Not right now."

There was no answer from the other side.

"Lex?"

"He's licking his balls, Connie," Tawny said with more than a little distaste. "I don't know exactly what he is, but I do know he is at least part cat. Gross!"

I laughed and opened the door. Tawny pulled me into a hug and Joe smooshed up against the both of us. We were an odd group, hugging in the hallway of the bed-and-breakfast I'd inherited from a complete stranger while a daemon cat sat licking his balls beside us.

CHAPTER 16

*S*he couldn't believe what she was hearing.

Maybelle drifted up, and down the hallway, pacing as she thought.

She had always been the evil twin and really enjoyed pretending to be Gladys all those years. Sure, it annoyed her that Gladys's ghost was still hanging around, but it was easy enough to bind her. She could see her at times, but that was all. It was easy to ignore.

Until the damn cat came along. Oh, that was sneaky. A tiny grey and white kitten, innocently left on her porch, mewing and crying for love.

Yes, she was a sucker. Into the house came Lex, and at the time, she had no idea she also allowed a daemon in.

That idiot Tawny was right when she told Connie about daemons. Sure, they were good and innocent and all that. But if they didn't like you, or if you crossed them, there was no telling what they might do to you. And apparently, Lex didn't like her.

Maybelle rolled her eyes. Lex had made her life a living hell. She knew he controlled some of her actions when she was alive. He whispered things to her in her sleep and then she would wake up and do them only to realize it later, when it was too late to change anything.

A perfect example was having Connie Keyes, and her friends stay at the house. Another one was leaving the house to her. She couldn't believe she had done that one.

But she thought she'd bested the little beast when a little research online told her all about Connie and where she worked. That led to who her family was and who her ancestors were, which led to a whole different plan.

Fine, she figured she would allow Connie to come to the house and appease Lex and whoever, or whatever else, wanted her there. But she would also manipulate the situation in order to get Connie to do her will. If she was going to bring a ghost whisperer and her friends into the house, she would use them to her advantage.

All she had to do was what she'd been doing for the last forty years. Tell the story of Gladys and Thomas and lead her to believe Maybelle was the evil ghost still hanging around. Then it would be simple to have her remove the spirit, leaving her free and clear to haunt and terrorize anyone who stepped foot into her house. Once she actually died, that is.

It would still be her house and no matter what the daemons wanted, whether Beezel in Charleston or Lex in Detroit, she would come out on top. They couldn't control her as a ghost.

Good grief, she was as much of a princess as Gladys was. Such prima donnas with their men to care for them. Maybelle never had and never needed, a man. She didn't want one either.

But now that she knew what they'd done, she panicked. What if they made her leave?

Better stick to her original threat and begin another reenactment.

~

We were relaxing in the sitting room. Lex agreed not to talk for a little while and just act like a cat. I was petting him while he purred, trying not to think about it too much.

We discussed the trauma of watching Gladys murdered and then Thomas dying right in front of us. No matter what we said, though, I knew Tawny wouldn't be prepared if she saw it.

"Just avoid the cellar," I suggested.

She readily agreed.

I also wondered why Lex and Beezel were still around even after the moratorium was lifted. We could look after ourselves now, yet they still stood guard.

I started to ask my question but was interrupted by a moaning and groaning Thomas drifting through the sitting room.

"Thomas! Where are you going? What's wrong?"

He didn't answer, but shook his head. His eyes were wide and frightened. He held his hands to his side helplessly.

"Follow him," Tawny suggested.

Despite having closed and locked the cellar door, Thomas drifted through it without hesitation. I quickly found the key and unlocked it.

"So much for avoiding the cellar," I said.

"Should we wait for Joe?" Tawny asked.

"I don't think we have time to get him."

He was back in Brodie. All the activity had taken a lot from him, and he said he needed to recoup his energies. I think he just wanted some alone time and I couldn't blame him.

We followed Thomas's spirit down the steps. He was still very nebulous and unformed, much as Joe was early on. We occasionally lost sight of him, even though he was right in front of us.

Sadly, what played out in front of us was as clear as day and somehow more horrible than before.

Tawny covered her mouth with her hand and stifled a scream as we witnessed Thomas watching Gladys die again, then Gladys watching Thomas witness her death and then relive his own death. Maybelle clapped her hands when it was over.

"What? No applause? Come on, that was great."

She drifted past us, causing us both to shiver.

Tawny took my hand and pulled me upstairs, where it was warm. She was locking the cellar door and jumped when the spirits of Thomas and Gladys emerged through the just closed door. They looked at us pointedly and then drifted away into the house.

I hoped they wouldn't run into Maybelle.

"This? This is what is supposed to happen over and over?"

I nodded as Tawny paced back and forth.

"Try to calm down," I suggested.

She looked at me with large, round eyes. "You're telling me to calm down? How can you be so calm? This is terrible Connie. No one can live like this. Stop going down there. If this happens again, don't follow Thomas. Stay away until we can figure something out. Promise me? This is horrid."

"Okay, I obviously agree with you. This was the second time, so it's not like I'm rushing to the cellar door every day."

Tawny spent most of the evening on the phone with Orenda and several other people whom I didn't know. She even asked for Madame's number, which I provided happily. She was gathering the troops, and they were devising a plan to remove Maybelle once and for all and put a stop to the daily horror show. They were moving quickly because Maybelle was gaining strength with every passing hour.

I hoped something would happen soon. Tawny was right. Even though I'd only witnessed it twice, it was devastating, and it invaded my dreams, turning them into nightmares.

I was preparing for a very early night, completely exhausted and upset. Joe had come out, and we told him what happened. He was upset that I'd experienced that again and without him. Even Lex was angry and stomped around my ankles all evening, refusing to leave my side.

Tawny was distraught, but she was working, which helped her process what she'd seen. The people she talked to provided a comfort for her and being busy was how she managed her distress. I tried to listen and glean as much as possible from what I could hear on my side of the conversations, but it was fruitless. All that happened was I got more and more upset and frustrated.

"How are you so calm?" I asked her between calls.

She smiled and held up a small tin.

"What's that?" I'd asked.

"Calms the nerves," she replied. "Here, take one."

I hesitated. I certainly drank, and back in my wild high school and college days, I may have dabbled with a few illicit items, but I hadn't taken anything that was not prescribed to me in a long while.

It didn't take long for me to decide, though. Lex wound himself between my legs and then sat in front of me.

"I'll watch over you. Take it."

166

When a talking daemon cat tells you to do something, you do it. So I took the pill and threw it back, chased with a tall glass of water.

Now, lying in bed, I could feel my muscles letting go. My mind finally stopped racing and drifted. I was warm and relaxed, with Lex curled against my right side. Then I felt the covers on my left moving and I reached over quickly.

"Shhhh, it's just me," Joe whispered. "Is this okay?"

"I didn't know you could do this," I murmured. "How are you under the covers? I can even feel you there."

"I don't know. Go to sleep. Lex and I are here."

I slept better that night than I had in ages.

CHAPTER 17

I awoke refreshed, relaxed, happy, and content for the first time in years. I rolled over and stretched as Lex matched my sigh with his own elongated body pressed to my side.

Joe was sitting up in the bed, looking at me.

"How long have been watching me? That's so creepy!"

"Not long. Don't worry, you only drooled a little. Your snoring, though. We might have to do something about that."

"Oh! You're one to talk," I swatted at his arm, completely forgetting for a moment that he was a ghost, and my hand went straight through to the bed.

The light mood disappeared. Was something wrong?

Reading my mind, Joe calmly said, "We both have to work on this. We can touch like we did last night, but we have to be intentional."

I nodded and then blushed when I wondered about something else.

Again, Joe read my mind. "I don't know about... other stuff. We can experiment sometime, if you want, that is."

As I struggled to wrap my mind around the concept and

wondered exactly how that could happen, a loud bang echoed throughout the house. We all jumped and Lex darted from the room.

"Now what?" I groused.

Joe and I followed quickly. We were met in the kitchen by Tawny, who was being dragged towards the cellar door by some unseen force. She was holding on for dear life to the kitchen table, but it was being dragged too.

"Help!" she said, reaching for my hand.

I grabbed her arm and tried to pull her back. No matter how hard I pulled, I could feel myself being sucked into the force that was pulling her towards the basement. Both of us lost the battle at the same time and barely caught ourselves before we tumbled down the stairs.

When we reached the bottom, Joe came up behind us and Lex sat a few steps away.

What began as a lovely morning turned into another hellish display as the drama once again unfolded before us.

Maybelle pranced around, acting out her part with glee and abandon while Gladys and Thomas looked on, miserable.

Then I noticed something. I attempted to return upstairs but was held to my spot until the spectacle was completed. After Maybelle brushed past us and retired upstairs, I turned to Tawny and Joe.

"Did you see it?"

Early that morning, while Joe and I languished in a shared bed, Tawny had attempted a spell given to her by one of Orenda's friends. Instead of binding Maybelle or stopping her at all, it simply sucked Tawny into the cycle as well.

Throughout the day, we saw Maybelle here and there.

She would stand in a corner, leaning against a wall, or be striding down a hallway.

I attempted to communicate with her, hoping to come to some sort of compromise. She refused to talk to me or even acknowledge my presence, except to remind me of her ultimatum. Either we removed Gladys and Thomas and killed Lex, or this was going to continue.

Her power baffled Tawny.

"She's a ghost. I don't know how she can do this. Joe, do you have any ideas? Lex?"

Both shook their heads. Lex admitted this was unlike anything he'd ever seen before and while he could influence her when she was alive, he had no control over her at all now.

And Joe readily admitted to being in way over his head. "I'm not that experienced as it is. There's no way I know anything about this."

Tawny pulled her phone from her back pocket and started punching keys. After several minutes, she looked up and smiled.

"The calvary is coming," she said. "Orenda and several others will be here in three days. We just have to sit tight until then."

"Three days? They can't make it any sooner?" I asked.

"Orenda refuses to fly. I've never been able to get her on a plane. They are driving."

While it was awful to witness, it was good to know the horror show would come to an end soon and we would have help. Ideally, in three days, we would put a stop to Maybelle's horrible reign over us all.

"So three more times? We can do this, right, guys?" I asked.

We all agreed we could manage it. One time a day for three more days. Tawny and I would do our best to resist going down to the cellar, but it seemed like we were sucked into the terrifying play, despite our resistance.

Unfortunately, Maybelle felt differently about it only being three more times. We were stunned when, for the second time that day, we were pulled towards the cellar door, thrust down the stairs and forced to witness the scene yet again.

I paid close attention this time, though. There was something I wanted to check, and I was thrilled to discover that what I thought I'd seen was correct.

It appeared each time the scene played out, Maybelle's clothes became more and more yellow and Gladys's more and more pink.

Also, Maybelle appeared younger each time. She died in her eighties, but with each replay she looked more and more like her twin at twenty-four.

We endured the rest of the torturous exhibition and then gathered on the front porch when it was over to dissect what we'd witnessed.

"What do you think it means?" I asked Tawny.

"I don't know, but you are right. After you mentioned it earlier, I watched closely. Their clothes are definitely changing and becoming brighter. And Maybelle's are changing from pink to yellow and she's getting younger."

"Great. Does that mean she's getting stronger?" Joe asked from Brodie's shoulder.

"I don't think so. In fact, I didn't feel as strong of a pull downstairs this time. Did you notice?"

"I did! But I thought I was imagining it," I said.

"Let's keep acting the same. Don't let on that we see anything different. Even if you think you can fight the pull to the cellar, don't. Just go with it until we figure out if we can get the upper hand."

~

Maybelle paced in front of the door. What were they talking about out there? And why couldn't she hear them or even open the door?

"Thomas!" she screamed his name. "Thomas!" Even louder this time, and he appeared in front of her.

"Don't make me call you twice," she growled at him. "You got yourself into this now you have to play your part. Go outside and find out what they are talking about."

"Maybelle, you know I can't go out there. I'm no different from you."

Maybelle rose to her full height and then lifted from the floor. She looked down at Thomas and bellowed. "You are nothing like me!"

As she attacked the shaking Thomas, Connie and the others entered the house. They were surprised by the spectacle occurring in the sitting room.

In the middle of the room floated a larger-than-life Maybelle. Her entire outfit was bright yellow and glowed all around her. Her hair was long and flowing, sparks flew from her fingertips. She slashed her fists through the air, landing them on Thomas each time.

Thomas cowered beneath the onslaught.

Everyone else shrank back. Something terrible had changed and the annoyance they thought they could live with for a few days became a desperate threat to them all. They no longer felt like they had the upper hand.

"Let's do it again, shall we?" Maybelle's voice boomed throughout the house.

She was delighted with her new powers. She wasn't certain she could pull off the second time earlier that day, but now she knew she could repeat the scene over and over as much as she wanted. She also knew no one could stop her.

"Come along." She sang out as she pulled the hapless prisoners behind her.

~

We were yanked along behind the most frightening apparition I'd ever seen. She was huge and bright, almost blindingly so. Electricity seemed to come from her image. Her eyes were wild and wide, her hair flowed from her head in all directions.

When we got to the cellar door, she flung it open with the twitch of her finger and descended the stairs.

We followed without choice and stood in our usual spots on the steps. Tawny and I side by side at the very bottom. Joe behind us and Lex behind him. Thomas was rooted in his assigned spot where he would once again watch the love of his life brutally murdered, only to find her remains and then relive his own death.

Gladys was sitting at the table waiting.

She looked up when we all appeared. Then the play began.

"I'm sorry they are sending you away," Gladys said.

"No, you're not. You're happy. Now you have everything for yourself. Thomas, our parents, the house. You've always wanted it all, and you've always had it all."

"How do I have it all? We are twins. We have the same parents, same house, the same looks. The only thing I have is Thomas, and you've done your best to take that away from me."

"You're right. I'm sorry," Maybelle moved closer to Gladys. "I don't want to go away," she whispered. "I'm scared."

"You need to go away, Maybelle. You've done enough damage here, and it's time to stop."

I heard Tawny inhale sharply. I looked at her. She shook her head slightly. I felt Joe's hands on my shoulders squeeze once. My heart beat so fast I was afraid I'd pass out.

"Those aren't the lines, Gladys. You're such an idiot. Do it again," Maybelle said through gritted teeth.

"Here, let me do your nails."

Gladys reached for the polish that sat between them, but Maybelle pulled her hands away.

"That's better. This won't go with yellow." She pushed herself from the tiny chair and collapsed back into it suddenly.

"I can't get up," she said, struggling to stand.

"Do you think anyone else ever comes down here?" Gladys asked. She stood and walked behind Maybelle.

"No, never. Just you and me. Why can't I get up? What's going on? Why are you walking around?"

"Remember playing down here? Like it was our own house? We'd use that old garden rake and pretend it was a broom? It was so heavy, neither of us could really lift it, but we'd still fight over who got to sweep."

She made another circle around the struggling Maybelle. As she walked, her own clothes grew more and more colorful until her pink was as bright and overwhelming as Maybelle's yellow.

"Look, Thomas. I have my pink back," Gladys said.

He nodded and smiled. Then he added, "Be careful, my pretty pink princess. That old rusty thing is still heavy and look how sharp. You're making rows in the dirt!"

She giggled. "I would have done this ages ago if I could have. You actually helped me by giving me back my love. With Thomas came my strength."

"Gladys, I don't know what you're thinking. Put the rake

174

down. Let's talk about it." Maybelle was alternating between holding her hands in front of her face and holding them over her head.

"Oh, Maybelle. I can't believe you didn't see this coming."

The rake landed on Maybelle's head and before she fell, Gladys was swinging again, chopping at the writhing form.

Rather than bleed, Maybelle disappeared. Small tendrils rose from her and then drifted away into nothingness. Soon, there was nothing left but the packed dirt floor.

Gladys stood in front of us. She held her hand out for Thomas, who rushed to her side.

Hand in hand, they climbed the stairs all the way to the very top, very pink, room in the tower.

CHAPTER 18

*T*awny left shortly after that day. There was no reason for her to hang around, and she still had her life in Charleston. I was grateful for her help here, but even more grateful when she taught Peyton and Hannah how to make peace with Beezel.

He'd finally stopped terrorizing them and seemed to understand what Orenda told him about them being my children and, therefore, under his protection. When Tawny arrived and explained to him about Lex and Detroit, he slowly understood. Still, I was nervous.

Lex commented again that Beezel wasn't the brightest daemon in the box and might need to hear the explanation a few more times.

Over the following weeks, we saw less and less of Gladys and Thomas. For a while we'd catch them holding hands and looking out a window or hovering close together in a random room. Neither one spoke to us, and only a few times did Gladys make eye contact with me, followed by a wink and a smile.

The look on their faces told the story of young love that endured the decades. They were a true love story, content with where they were right now, content to be together no matter how.

"I haven't seen the lovebirds lately," Joe said as I settled onto the couch beside him. Lex had taken over my favorite chair, but that was okay. I wanted to sit with Joe.

"I haven't either. We see less and less of them, it seems. I wonder why?"

"They probably don't want to see us. They only have eyes for each other. Remember that? Young love?"

"Were we ever like that?" I asked as I snuggled under his arm and felt the warm weight of his body.

"Tawny said we were a love story, remember?"

"Yeah, but she's a kid. What does she know? I don't know what this is, but I like it."

"If this is a love story, I wish it had started sooner," Joe said.

"Let's not dwell on the past. Let's go forward from where we are now. People form relationships in all walks of life and couples can be anything. Even a person and a ghost can be happily married."

I rested my head on his shoulder and sighed. It was nice to have him back, regardless of the form. It was as though we had a new marriage and a new life. I relaxed for the first time in a very long while and felt like I had my partner back. Only this time, he was really and truly back.

Lex stretched and scratched his claws on the chair.

"Lex! Stop it! You have a post for that."

He completely ignored me and went right on scratching.

"More and more like a cat every day, buddy. Watch yourself."

Joe laughed and Lex, apparently satisfied with the fluffiness of the chair now, curled into a ball and fell back asleep.

I sighed. "Let's watch something." I reached for the remote control.

"Wait, I've got it," Joe said. "Look what I learned."

And he began making the TV change channels.

I had my husband back, but I still didn't have control of the remote.

Unexpected reservations, ghostly guests, fighting brothers, and a neutered Lex? See what's coming up next for Connie and crew in Picking Locks: Book 3 in the Extra-Ordinary Midlife series. Coming Spring 2022. Click here to preorder!

Drawing by Blake Stout. Find her on Twitter @lettucefight

ALSO BY LYNN M. STOUT

Paranormal Women's Fiction

Breaking Locks

She's recently widowed and on the wrong side of fifty. Seeing dead people wasn't her idea of a midlife reinvention.

Changing Locks

Quietly exploring her newfound abilities and reinventing her life, she discovers fifty is the new forty ... and there's nothing quiet about it.

Picking Locks

Talking cats, surprise guests, and ghosts galore. It's a midlife revival!

Dead Locks

Coming Fall 2022

Paranormal Thrillers

Evil Follows

The evil should have perished in the fire. Instead, it followed her home.

The Unheard

Her cat is possessed. She sees murders in her dreams. She might be married to a serial killer.

Once Again

Jody protects everyone, but this time, she's the one in the crosshairs.

NOTE FROM THE AUTHOR

Thank you for reading.

If you enjoyed this book, please consider leaving a review at your favorite book review site. It helps other readers decide if they'd like to read the book and it is one of the best ways to support indie authors.

I'd love to stay in touch. Be sure to sign up for monthly newsletter updates. You'll receive exclusive bonus content and be among the first to preorder the next book in the Extra-Ordinary Midlife series!

Visit www.lynnstout.com for more information.

facebook.com/lstoutwrites

twitter.com/lstoutwrites

instagram.com/lstoutwrites

Made in the USA
Middletown, DE
18 July 2022